Earth's Last Fortress

and

The Three Eyes of Evil

A. E. VAN VOGT

SPHERE BOOKS LIMITED
30/32 Gray's Inn Road, London WC1X 8JL

First published in Great Britain
by Sidgwick & Jackson Ltd. 1973
under the title *The Three Eyes of Evil*
Earth's Last Fortress copyright © Ace Books Inc. 1969
The Three Eyes of Evil copyright © Ace Books Inc.
1959

First Sphere Books edition 1977

TRADE MARK

Set in Linotype Pilgrim

Printed in Great Britain by
C. Nicholls & Company Ltd
The Philips Park Press, Manchester

WELCOME TO THE FUTURE . . .

The machine was coming swiftly, monstrously
alive. It glowed with a soft, swelling white
light, and then seemed to burst into an
enormous flame. A breaker of writhing
tongues of blue and green and red and yellow
fire stormed over that first glow, blotting it
from view instantaneously. The fire sprayed
and flashed with a wild and violent beauty,
a glittering blaze of unearthly glory.
And then – just like that – the flame faded
and was gone. The machine was again a mass
of inert metallic deadness. And the recruit
who had stepped into the room had vanished.
Dr. Lell appeared in the doorway, and Norma
stared at him, licking dry lips.
"W – what happened to that man?"
His voice was cool, amused. "Why, he went
out the back door."

Earth's
Last Fortress

CHAPTER ONE

She didn't dare! Suddenly, the night was a cold, enveloping thing. The edge of the broad, black river gurgled evilly at her feet as if, now that she had changed her mind, it hungered for her.

Her foot slipped on the wet, sloping ground, and her thoughts grew blurred with the terrible, senseless fear that *things* were reaching out of the night, trying to drown her now against her will. She fought her way up the bank and slumped, breathlessly, onto the nearest park bench. Dully, she watched the gaunt man come along the pathway past the light standard. So sluggish was her mind that she was not aware of surprise when she realized he was coming straight toward her.

The purulent yellowish light made a crazy patch of his shadow across her where she sat. His voice, when he spoke, was vaguely foreign in tone, yet modulated, cultured. He said, 'Are you interested in the Calonian cause?'

Norma stared. There was no quickening in her brain, but suddenly she began to laugh. It was funny, horribly, hysterically funny. To be sitting here, trying to get up the nerve for another attempt at those deadly waters, and then to have some crackbrain come along and –

'You're deluding yourself, Miss Matheson,' the man went on coolly. 'You're not the suicide type.'

'Nor the pickup type!' She answered automatically. 'Beat it before –'

Abruptly, it penetrated that the man had called her by name. She looked up sharply at the dark blank that was his face. His head against the background of distant light nodded as if in reply to the question that quivered in her thought.

'Yes, I know your name. I also know your history and your fear.'

'What do you mean?'

'I mean that a young scientist named Garson arrived in the city tonight to deliver a series of lectures. Ten years ago, when you and he graduated from the same university, he asked you to marry him, but you wanted a career. And now you're terrified that in your extremity you might turn to him for assistance.'

'Stop!'

The man seemed to watch her as she sat there breathing heavily. He said at last, quietly, 'I think I have proved that I am not simply a casual philanderer.'

'What other kind of philanderer is there?' Norma asked, sluggish again. But she made no objection as he sank down on the far end of the bench. His back was still to the light, his features night-enveloped.

'Ah,' he said, 'you joke. You are bitter. But that is an improvement. You feel now, perhaps, that if somebody has taken an interest in you, all is not lost.'

Norma said dully, 'People who are acquainted with the basic laws of psychology are cursed with the memory of them, even when disaster strikes into their lives. All I've done the last ten years is –' She stopped, then : 'You're very clever. Without more than arousing a mild suspicion, you've insinuated yourself into the company of an hysterical woman. What's your purpose?'

'I intend to offer you a job.'

Norma's laugh sounded so harsh in her own ears that she thought, startled, *I am hysterical!* Aloud, she said, 'An apartment, jewels, a car of my own, I suppose?'

His reply was cool. 'No. To put it frankly, if I were looking for a mistress, I'd pass you by. You are not pretty enough as you are right now. Too angular, mentally and physically. That's been one of your troubles the last ten years : developing introversion of the mind which has influenced the shape of your body unfavourably.'

The words shivered through the suddenly stiffened muscles of her body. With an enormous effort, she forced herself to relax. She said, 'I had that coming to me. Insults are good for hysteria. So now what?'

'Are you interested in the Calonian cause?'

'There you go again,' she complained. 'But, yes, I'm for it. Birds of a feather, you know.'

'I know very well indeed. In fact, in those words you named the reason why I am here tonight, hiring a young woman who is up against it. Calonia, too, is up against it and –' He stopped. In the darkness, he spread his shadowlike hands. 'You see : good publicity for our recruiting centers.'

Norma nodded. It seemed to her that she did see, and

suddenly she didn't trust herself to speak. Her hand trembled as she took the key he held out.

'This key,' he said, 'will fit the lock of the front door leading to the apartment above the center. The apartment is yours while you have the job. You can go there tonight if you wish, or wait until morning if you fear this is merely a device. Now, I must give you a warning.'

'Warning?'

'Yes. The work we are doing is illegal. Actually, only the American government can enlist American citizens and operate recruiting stations. We exist on sufferance and sympathy, but at any time someone may lay a charge and the police will have to act.'

Norma nodded rapidly. 'That's no risk,' she said. 'No judge would ever –'

'The address is 322 Carlton Street,' he cut in smoothly. 'And for your information, my name is Dr. Lell.'

Norma had the distinct sense of being pushed along too swiftly for caution. She hesitated, her mind on the street address. 'Is that near Bessemer?'

It was his turn to hesitate. 'I'm afraid,' he confessed, 'I don't know this city very well, at least not in its twentieth century. You see,' he finished suavely, 'I was here many years ago, around the mid-century.'

Norma wondered vaguely why he bothered to explain. She said half-accusingly, 'You're not a Calonian. You sound – French, maybe.'

'You're not a Calonian either,' he said, and stood up abruptly. She watched his great gloom-wrapped figure walk off into the night and vanish.

CHAPTER TWO

She stopped short in the deserted night street. The sound that came was like a whisper touching her brain; a machine whirring somewhere with a soft humming sound. For a moment, her mind concentrated on the shadow vibrations; and then, somehow, they seemed to fade like figments of her imagination. Suddenly, there was only the street and the silent night. The street was dimly lighted, and that brought doubt, sharp and tinged with fear. She strained her eyes and traced the numbers on the doors until she came to 322. That was it! The place was in darkness. She peered at the signs that made up the window display:

FIGHT FOR THE BRAVE CALONIANS!
THE CALONIANS ARE FIGHTING FREEDOM'S
FIGHT — YOUR FIGHT! IF YOU CAN PAY YOUR
OWN WAY, IT WOULD BE APPRECIATED
OTHERWISE WE'LL GET YOU OVER!

There were other signs, but they were essentially the same, all terribly honest and appealing if you really thought about the desperate things that made up their grim background. Illegal, of course. But the man had admitted that, too. With sudden end of doubt, she took the key from her purse.

There were two doorways, one on either side of the window. The one to the right led into the recruiting station. The one on the left led up dimly lighted stairs. The apartment at the top was uninhabited. The door had a bolt. She clicked it home, and then, wearily, headed for the bedroom. It was as she lay in the bed that she grew aware again of the faint whirring of a machine. It was a mere whisper of sound, and, queerly, it seemed to reach into her brain. The very last second before she drifted into sleep, the pulse of the vibration, remote as the park bench, was a steady beat inside her.

All through the night that faint whirring was there. Only occasionally did it seem to be in her head. She was aware of turning, twisting, curling, straightening and, in the fractional wakefulness that accompanied each move, the tiniest vibrational tremors would sweep down along her nerves like infinitesimal currents of energy.

Spears of sunlight, piercingly brilliant through the small window, brought her awake at last. She lay taut and strained for a moment and then relaxed, puzzled. There was not a sound from the maddening machine, only the raucous noises of the awakening street. She found food in the refrigerator and in the little pantry. The weariness of the night vanished swiftly before the revivifying power of breakfast. She thought with gathering interest, *What did he look like, that strange-voiced man of night?*

Relief flooded her when the key unlocked the door to the recruiting room, for there had been in her mind a fear that this was all quite mad. She shuddered the darkness out of her system. The world was sunlit and cheerful, not the black and gloomy abode of people with angular introversion of the mind.

She flushed at the memory of the words. There was no pleasure in knowing that the man's clever analysis of her was true. Still stinging, she examined the little room. There were four chairs, a bench, a long wooden counter; newspaper clippings of the Calonian War were tacked up on the otherwise bare walls. There was a back door to the place. Curious, she tried the knob – once! It was locked, but there was something about the feel of it that shocked her. The door, in spite of its wooden appearance, was solid metal.

The chill of that discovery finally left her. She thought, *None of my business.* And then, before she could turn away, the door opened and a gaunt man loomed on the threshold. He snapped harshly, almost into her face, 'Oh, yes, it is your business!'

It was not fear that made her back away. The deeps of her mind registered the cold voice, so different from that of the previous night. She was aware of the ugly sneer on his face. But there was no real emotion in her, nothing but a blurred blankness. It wasn't fear. It couldn't be fear because all she had to do was run a few yards and she'd be out on a busy street. And besides, she had never before been afraid of people who had the misfortune of not looking quite human, and she wasn't now.

That first impression that he wasn't quite human was so sharp, so immensely surprising, that the fast-following second impression seemed like a trick of her eyes. For the man was actually just foreign looking. She shook her head, trying to shake that trickiness out of her vision. But the picture remained steady now. He wasn't colored, he wasn't white but he was a combination of types and races. Slowly, her brain adjusted itself to his alienness. She saw that he had slant eyes like a Chinese. His skin, though dark, was fine in texture, but it was not a young face. The nose was sheer chiseled beauty, the most handsome, most normal part of his face. His mouth was thin-lipped, commanding; his bold chin gave strength and power to the insolence of his steel-gray eyes. His sneer deepened.

'Oh, no,' he said softly, 'you're not afraid of me, are you? Let me inform you that my purpose is to make you afraid. Last night I had the purpose of bringing you here. That required tact, understanding. My new purpose requires, among other things, the realization on your part that you are in my power beyond the control of your will or wish. I could have allowed you to discover gradually that this is not a Calonian recruiting station. But I prefer to get these early squirmings of the slaves over as soon as possible. The reaction to the power of the machine is always so similar and unutterably boring.'

'I – I don't understand!'

He answered coldly, 'Let me be brief. You have been vaguely aware of a machine. That machine has attuned the rhythm of your body to itself, and through its actions I can control you against your desire. Naturally, I don't expect you to believe me. Like other women, you will test its mind-destroying power. Notice that I said *women!* We always hire women. For purely psychological reasons, they are safer than men. You will discover what I mean if you should attempt to warn any applicant on the basis of what I have told you.' He finished swiftly, 'Your duties are simple. There is a pad on the table made up of sheets with simple questions printed on them. Ask those questions, note the answers, then direct the applicants to me in the back room. I have – er – a medical examination to give them.'

Of all the things he had said, the one that searingly dominated her whole mind had no connection with her personal fate. 'But,' she gasped, 'if these men are not being sent to Calonia, where –'

His hiss of caution cut her words short. 'Here comes a man. Now, remember!'

He stepped back to one side, out of sight in the dimness of the back room. Behind her there was the dismaying sound of the front door opening. A man's baritone voice blurred a greeting into her ears.

Her fingers shook as she wrote down the man's answers to the dozen questions. Name, address, next of kin . . . His face was a ruddy-cheeked blur against the shapeless, shifting pattern of her racing thoughts. 'You can see,' she heard herself mumbling, 'that these questions are only a matter of identification. Now, if you'll go into the back room –'

The sentence shattered into silence. She'd said it! The uncertainty of her mind, the unwillingness to take a definite stand until she had thought of some way out, had made her say the very thing she had intended to avoid.

The man said, 'What do I go in there for?'

She stared at him numbly. Her mind felt sick, useless. She needed time, calm. She said at last, 'It's a simple medical exam, entirely for your own protection.'

Sickly, Norma watched his stocky form head briskly toward the rear door. He knocked, and the door opened. Surprisingly, it stayed open. Surprisingly, because it was then, as the man disappeared from her line of vision, that she saw the machine. The immense and darkly gleaming end of it that she could see reared up halfway to the ceiling, partially hiding a door that seemed to be a rear exit from the building.

She forgot the door, forgot the man. Her mind fastened on the great machine as swift realization came that *this* was the machine. Involuntarily, her body, her ears, her mind strained for the whirring sound that she had heard in the night. But there was nothing, not a whisper, not the tiniest of tiny noises, not the vaguest stir of vibration. The machine crouched there, hugging the floor with its solidness, its clinging metal strength; and it was dead, motionless.

The doctor's smooth, persuasive voice came to her, 'I hope you don't mind going out the back door, Mr. Barton. We ask applicants to use it because – well, our recruiting station is illegal. As you probably know, we exist on sufferance and sympathy, but we don't want to be too blatant about the success we're having in getting young men to fight for our cause.'

Norma waited. As soon as the man was gone she would force a showdown on this whole fantastic affair. If this was some distorted scheme of Calonia's enemies, she would go to the police immediately. The thought twisted into a swirling chaos of wonder.

The machine was coming swiftly, monstrously alive. It glowed with a soft, swelling white light, and then seemed to burst into an enormous flame. A breaker of writhing tongues of blue and green and red and yellow fire stormed over that first glow, blotting it from view instantaneously. The fire sprayed and flashed like an intricately designed fountain, with a wild and violent beauty, a glittering blaze of unearthly glory.

And then – just like that – the flame faded. Briefly, stubborn in its fight for life, the swarming, sparkling energy clung to the metal. It was gone. The machine lay there a mass of metallic deadness, inert, motionless. The doctor appeared in the doorway.

'Sound chap,' he said, satisfaction in his tone. 'Heart requires a bit of glandular adjustment to eradicate the effects of bad diet. Lungs will react swiftly to gas-immunization injections, and our surgeons should be able to patch that body up from almost anything except an atomic storm.'

Norma licked dry lips. 'What are you talking about?' she asked wildly. 'W – what happened to that man?'

She was aware of him staring at her blandly. His voice was cool, amused. 'Why, he went out the back door.'

'He did not! He –'

She realized the uselessness of words. Cold with the confusion of her thought, she emerged from behind the counter. She brushed past him, and then, as she reached the threshold of the door leading into the rear room, her knees wobbled. She grabbed at the doorjamb for support, and knew that she didn't dare go near that machine. With an effort she said, 'Will you go over there and open it?'

He did so, smiling. The door squealed slightly as it opened. When he closed it, it creaked, and the automatic lock clicked loudly. There had been no such sound. Norma felt the deepening whiteness in her cheeks. Chilled, she asked, 'What is this machine?'

'Owned by the local electric company, I believe,' he answered suavely, and his voice mocked her. 'We just have permission to use the room, of course.'

'That's not possible,' she said thickly. 'Electrical companies don't have machines in the back rooms of shabby buildings.'

He shrugged. 'Really,' he said indifferently, 'this is beginning to bore me. I have already seen some of its powers, yet your mind persists in being practical after a twentieth-century fashion. I will repeat merely that you are a slave of the machine, and that it will do no good to go to the police, entirely aside from the fact that I saved you from suicide by drowning, and gratitude alone should make you realize that you owe everything to me, and nothing to the world you were prepared to desert. However, that is too much to expect. You will learn by experience.'

Quite calmly, Norma walked across the room. She opened the door, and then, startled that he had made no move to stop her, turned to stare at him. He was still standing there, and he was smiling.

'You must be quite mad,' she said after a moment. 'Perhaps you had some idea that your little trick, whatever it was, would put the fear of the unknown into me. Let me dispel that right now. I'm going to the police this very minute.'

The picture that remained in her mind as she climbed aboard the bus was of him standing there, tall and casual and terrible in his contemptuous derision. The chill of that memory slowly mutilated the steady tenor of her forced calm.

CHAPTER THREE

The sense of nightmare vanished as she climbed off the streetcar in front of the imposing police building. Sunshine splashed vigorously on the pavement, cars honked. The life of the city swirled lustily around her, and brought a wave of returning confidence.

The answer, now that she thought of it, was simplicity itself. Hypnotism! That was what had made her see a great, black, unused engine burst into mysterious flames. Tingling with anger at the way she had been tricked, she lifted her foot to step on the curb.

The foot, instead of lifting springily, dragged. Her muscles almost refused to carry the weight. She grew aware of a man less than a dozen feet from her, staring at her with popping eyes.

'Good heavens!' he gasped audibly. 'I must be seeing things.'

He walked off rapidly, and the part of her thoughts that registered his odd actions tucked them away. She felt too weary, mentally and physically, even for curiosity. With faltering steps she moved across the sidewalk. It was as if something was tearing at her strength, holding her with invisible but immense forces. *The machine!* she thought, and panic blazed through her.

Will power kept her going. She reached the top of the steps and approached the big doors. It was then the first sick fear came that she couldn't make it; and as she strained feebly against the hard resistance of the door, the fever of dismay grew hot and terrible inside her. What had happened to her? How could a machine reach out over a distance and strike unerringly at one particular individual with such enormous devitalizing power?

A shadow leaned over her. The booming voice of a policeman who had just come up the steps was the most heartening sound she'd ever heard. 'Too much for you, eh, madam? Here, I'll push that door for you.'

'Thank you,' she said, and her voice sounded so weak and unnatural in her own ears that a new terror flared. In a few minutes she wouldn't be able to speak above a whisper.

16

'A slave of the machine,' he had said, and she knew with a clear and burning logic that if she was ever to conquer, it was now. She must get into this building. She must see someone in authority, and she must tell him . . . must . . . must . . . Somehow, she pumped strength into her brain and courage into her heart and forced her legs to carry her across the threshold into the big modern building with its mirrored anteroom and its fine marble corridors. Inside, she knew suddenly that she had reached her limit. She stood there on the hard floor and felt her whole body shaking from the enormous effort it took simply to stay erect. Her knees felt dissolved and cold, like ice turning to liquid. She grew aware that the big policeman was hovering uncertainly beside her.

'Anything I can do, mother?' he asked heartily.

Mother! she echoed mentally with a queer sense of insanity. Her mind skittered off after the word. Did he really say that, or had she dreamed it? Why, she wasn't a mother. She wasn't even married.

She fought the thought off. She'd have to pull herself together, or there was madness here. No chance now of getting to an inspector or an officer. The big constable must be her confidant, her hope to defeat the mighty power that was striking at her across miles of city, an incredibly evil, terrible power whose ultimate purpose she could not begin to imagine. She parted her lips to speak, and it was then she saw the mirror.

She saw a tall, thin, old, old woman standing beside the fresh-cheeked bulk of a blue-garbed policeman. It was such an abnormal trick of vision that it fascinated her. In some way, the mirror was missing her image and reflecting instead the form of an old woman who must be close behind and slightly to one side of her. She half-lifted her red-gloved hand toward the policeman to draw his attention to the distortion. Simultaneously, the red-gloved hand of the old woman in the mirror reached toward the policeman. Her own raised hand stiffened in midair; so did the hand of the old woman. Puzzled, she drew her gaze from the mirror and stared blankly at that rigidly uplifted hand. A tiny bit of wrist was visible between her glove and the sleeve of her woolen suit. Her skin wasn't really so dark as that!

Two things happened then. A tall man came softly through the door – Dr. Lell – and the big policeman's hand touched her shoulder.

'Really, madam, at your age, you shouldn't come here. A phone call would serve.'

And Dr. Lell was saying, 'My poor old grandmother –'

Their voices went on, but the sense of them jangled in her brain as she jerked frantically to pull the glove off a hand wrinkled and shriveled by age. Blackness, pierced with agonized splinters of light, reached mercifully into her brain. Her very last thought was that it must have happened just before she stepped onto the curb, when the man had stared at her pop-eyed and thought himself crazy. He must have seen the change taking place.

The pain faded; the blackness turned gray, then white. She was conscious of a car engine purring, and of forward movement. She opened her eyes – and her brain reeled from a surge of awful memory.

'Don't be afraid,' said Dr. Lell, and his voice was as soothing and gentle as it had been hard and satirical at the recruiting station. 'You are again yourself. In fact, you are approximately ten years younger.'

He removed one hand from the steering wheel and flashed a mirror before her eyes. The brief glimpse she had of her image made her grab at the silvered glass as if it were the most precious thing in all the world.

One long hungry look she took. And then her arm, holding the mirror, collapsed to the seat. Tears sticky on her cheeks, weak and sick from reaction, she lay back against the cushions. At last she said steadily, 'Thanks for telling me right away. Otherwise I should have gone mad.'

'That, of course, was why I told you,' he said. His voice was still soft, still calm. And she felt soothed, in spite of the dark terror just past, in spite of the intellectual realization that this diabolical man used words and tones and human emotions as coldly as Pan himself piping his reed, sounding what stop he pleased. That quiet, deep voice went on : 'You see, you are now a valuable member of our twentieth-century staff, with a vested interest in the success of our purpose. You thoroughly understand the system of rewards and punishments for good or bad service. You will have food, a roof over your head, money to spend – and eternal youth! Woman, look at your face again, look hard, and rejoice at your good fortune. Weep for those who have nothing but old age and death as their future. Look hard, I say!'

18

It was like gazing at a marvelous photograph out of the past, except that she had been somewhat prettier in the actuality, her face more rounded, not so sharp, more girlish. She was twenty again, but different, more mature, leaner. She heard his voice go on dispassionately, a distant background to her own thoughts, feeding, feeding at the image in the mirror.

'As you can see,' Dr. Lell said, 'you are not truly yourself as you were at twenty. This is because we could only manipulate the time tensions which influenced your thirty-year-old according to the rigid mathematical laws governing the energies and forces involved. We could not undo the harm wrought these last rather prim, introverted years of your life because you have already lived them, and nothing can change that.'

It came to her that he was talking to give her time to recover from the deadliest shock that had ever stabbed into a human brain. And for the first time she thought, not of herself, but of the incredible things implied by every action that had occurred, every word spoken.

'Who are you?'

He was silent. The car twisted in and out of the clamorous traffic, and she watched his face now, that lean, strange, dark, finely chiseled, *evil* face with its glittering dark eyes. For the moment she felt no repulsion, only a gathering fascination at the way that strong chin tilted unconsciously as he said in a cold, proud, ringing voice, 'We are the masters of time. We live at the farthest frontier of time itself, and all the ages belong to us. No words could begin to describe the vastness of our empire or the futility of opposing us.' He stopped. Some of the fire faded from his dark eyes. His brows knit, his chin dropped, his lips clamped into a thin line, then parted as he snapped, 'I hope that any ideas you have had for further opposition will yield to the logic of events and of fact. Now you know why we hire women who have no friends.'

'You devil!' She half-sobbed the words.

'Ah,' he said softly. 'I can see you understand a woman's psychology. Two final points should clinch the argument I am trying to make. First, I can read your mind, every thought that comes into it, every emotion that moves it. And second, before establishing the machine in that particular building, we explored the years to come; and during all the time investigated, found the machine unharmed, its presence unsuspected by those in authority. Therefore, the future record is that you did nothing! I think you will agree that this is convincing.'

Norma nodded dully, her mirror forgotten. 'Yes,' she said, 'yes, I suppose it is.'

CHAPTER FOUR

Miss Norma Matheson
Calonian Recruiting Station
322 Carlton Street
Dear Norma :

I made a point of addressing the envelope of this letter to you c/o General Delivery, instead of the above address. I would not care to put you in any danger, however imaginary. I use the word imaginary deliberately for I cannot begin to describe how grieved and astounded I was to receive such a letter from the girl I once loved – it's eleven years since I proposed on graduation day, isn't it? – and how amazed I was by your questions and statements about time travel.

I might say that if you are not already mentally unbalanced, you will be shortly unless you take hold of yourself. The very fact that you were nerving yourself to commit suicide when this man – Dr. Lell – hired you from a park bench to be clerk in the recruiting station, is evidence of hysteria. You could have gone on city relief.

I see that you have lost none of your powers of self-expression. Your letter, mad though it is in subject matter, is eminently coherent and well thought out. Your drawing of the face of Dr. Lell is a remarkable piece of work.

If it is a true resemblance, then I agree that he is definitely not, shall I say, Western. His eyes are distinctly slanted, like the Chinese. You show the skin to be dark, indicating a faint Negro strain. His nose is very fine and sensitive, strong in character.

This effect is incremented by his mouth, though those thin lips are much too arrogant – the whole effect is of an extraordinarily intelligent man, a supermongrel in appearance. Such people could probably be produced in the southeastern provinces of Asia.

I pass without comment over your description of the machine which swallows up the unsuspecting recruits. The superman has apparently not objected to answering your questions since the police station incident; and so we have a new theory of time and space.

Time, he states, is the all, the only reality. Every unfolding instant the Earth and its life, the universe and all its galaxies are re-created by the titanic energy that is time. And always it is essentially the same pattern that is re-formed, because that is the easiest course.

He makes a comparison. According to Einstein, and in this he is correct, the Earth goes around the Sun, not because there is such a force as gravitation, but because it is easier for it to go around the Sun in exactly the way it does than to hurtle off into space.

It is easier for time to re-form the same pattern of rock, the same man, the same tree, the same earth. That is all; that is the law.

The rate of reproduction is approximately ten billion a second. During the past minute, therefore, six hundred billion replicas of myself have been created; and all of them are still there, each a separate body occupying its own space, completely unaware of the others. Not one has been destroyed. There is no purpose; it is simply easier to let them stay there than to destroy them.

If those bodies ever met in the same space – that is, if I should go back and shake hands with my twenty-year-old self there would be a clash of similar patterns, and the interloper would be distorted out of memory and shape.

I have no criticism of this theory to make, other than that it is utterly fantastic. However, it is very interesting in the vivid picture it draws of an eternity of human beings, breeding and living and dying in the quiet eddies of the time stream, while the great current flares on ahead in a fury of incredible creation.

I am puzzled by the detailed information you are seeking – you make it almost seem real – but I give the answers for what they are worth:

1. Time travel would naturally be based on the most rigid mechanical laws.

2. It seems plausible that they would be able to investigate your future actions.

3. Dr. Lell used phrases such as 'atomic storm' and 'gas-immunization injections.' The implication is that they are recruiting for an unimaginably great war.

4. I cannot see how the machine could act on you over a distance – unless there was some sort of radio-controlled intermediate. In your position, I would ask myself one

question: Was there anything, any metal, anything, upon my person that might have been placed there by an enemy?
5. Some thoughts are so dimly held that they could not possibly be transmitted. Presumably, sharp, clear thoughts might be receivable. If you could keep your mind calm, as you say you did while deciding to write the letter – the letter itself is proof that you succeeded.
6. It is unwise to assume that here is greater basic intelligence; but rather greater development of the potential forces of the mind. If men ever learn to read minds, it will be because they train their innate capacity for mind reading; they will be clever only when new knowledge adds new techniques of training.

To become personal, I regret immeasurably having heard from you. I had a memory of a rather brave spirit, rejecting my proposal of marriage, determined to remain independent, ambitious for advancement in the important field of social services. Instead, I find a sorry ending, a soul degenerated, a mind feeding on fantasia and a sense of incredible persecution. My advice is: go to a psychiatrist before it is too late, and to that end I enclose a money order for $200, and extend you my best wishes.

Yours in memory,
Jack Garson

At least there was no interference with her private life. No footsteps but her own ever mounted the dark, narrow flight of stairs that led to her tiny apartment. At night, after the recruiting shop closed, she walked the crowded streets. Sometimes, there was a movie that seemed to promise surcease from the deadly strain of living. Sometimes a new book on her old love, the social sciences, held her for a brief hour.

But there was nothing, absolutely nothing, that could relax the burning pressure of the reality of the machine. It was always there, like a steel band drawn tautly around her mind.

It was crazy funny to read about the Calonian War, and the victories and the defeats, when somewhere in the future an even greater war was being fought; a war so great that all the ages were being ransacked for manpower. And men came! Dark men, blond men, young men, grim men, hard men, and veterans of other wars. The stream of them was a steady flow into that dimly lighted back room. And one day she looked up from an intent, mindless study of the pattern of the stained old counter, and there was Jack Garson!

He leaned on the counter, not much older looking after ten years, a little leaner of face perhaps, and there were tired lines around his dark eyes. While she stared at him in dumb paralysis, he said, 'I had to come, of course. You were the first emotional tie I had, and also the last. When I wrote that letter, I didn't realize how strong that emotion still is. What's all this about?'

She thought with a flaming intensity: Often in the past, Dr. Lell had vanished for brief periods during the day hours. Once, she had seen him disappear into the flamboyant embrace of the light shed by the machine. Twice, she had opened the door of his room to speak to him, and found him gone.

All accidental observations! It meant he had stepped scores of times into his own world when she hadn't seen him.

Please let this be one of the times when he was away.

A second thought came, so fierce, so sharply focused that it made a pain inside her head. She must be calm. She must hold her mind away from giveaway thoughts, if it was not already ages too late.

Her voice came into the silence like a wounded, fluttering bird, briefly stricken by shock, then galvanized by agony. 'Quick! You must go – till after six. Hurry!'

Her trembling hands struck at his chest, as if by her blows she would set him running for the door. But the thrust of her strength was lost on the muscles of his breast, defeated by the way he was leaning forward. His body did not even stagger.

Through a blur, she saw he was staring down at her with a grim, set smile. His voice was hard as chipped steel as he said, 'Somebody's certainly thrown a scare into you. But don't worry – I've got a revolver in my pocket. And don't think I'm alone in this. I wired the Calonian Embassy at Washington; then notified the police here of their answer. They have no knowledge of this place. The police will arrive in minutes. I came in first to see that you didn't get hurt in the shuffle. Come on, outside with you, because –'

It was Norma's eyes that must have warned him – her eyes glaring past him. She was aware of him whirling to face the dozen men who were trooping out of the back room. The men came stolidly, and she had time to see that they were short, squat, ugly creatures, more roughly built than the

24

lean, finely molded Dr. Lell; and their faces were not so much evil as half dead with unintelligence.

A dozen pairs of eyes lighted with brief, animal-like curiosity as they stared at the scene outside the window. Then they glanced indifferently at her and at Jack Garson and the revolver he was holding so steadily. Finally, their interest fading visibly, their gazes reverted expectantly to Dr. Lell, who stood smiling laconically on the threshold of the doorway.

'Ah, yes, Professor Garson, you have a gun, haven't you? And the police are coming. Fortunately, I have something here that may convince you of the uselessness of your puny plans.'

His hand came from behind his back, where he had been hiding it. A gasp escaped from Norma as she saw that in it he held a blazing ball, a globe of furious flame, a veritable ball of fire. The thing burned there in his palm, crude and terrible in the illusion of incredible, destroying incandescence. The mockery in Dr. Lell's voice was utterly convincing, as he said in measured tones to her, 'My dear Miss Matheson, I think you will agree that you will not offer further obstacles to our purpose, now that we have enlisted this valuable young man into the invincible armies of the Glorious – and as for you, Garson, I suggest you drop that gun before it burns off your hand.'

His words were lost in the cry that came from Jack Garson. Amazed, Norma saw the gun fall to the floor, and lie there burning with a white hot intensity. Garson stared at the weapon; he seemed enthralled, unmindful of danger, as it shrank visibly in that intense fire. In seconds, there was no weapon, no metal; the fire blinked out. The floor where the gun had lain was not even singed.

From Dr. Lell came a barked command, oddly twisted, foreign-sounding words that nevertheless must have meant: *'Grab him!'*

She looked up, abruptly sick; but there was no fight. Jack Garson did not resist as the wave of beast men flowed around him. Dr. Lell said, 'So far, Professor, you haven't made a very good showing as a gallant rescuer. But I'm glad to see that you have already recognized the hopelessness of opposing us. It is possible that, if you remain reasonable, we will not have to destroy your personality. And now' – urgency sharpened his tone – 'I had intended to wait and capture your burly policemen; but as they have not arrived at the proper moment – a tradition with them, I believe – I think we shall have to go without them. It's just as well, I suppose.'

He waved his hands that held the ball of fire, and the men carrying Jack Garson literally ran into the back room. Almost instantly, they were out of sight. Norma had a brief glimpse of the machine blazing into radiance. And then there was only Dr. Lell striding forward, leaning over the bench, his eyes narrowed with menace.

'Go upstairs instantly! I don't think the police will recognize you – but if you make one false move, *he* will pay. Go quickly!'

As she hurried past the window, she saw his tall figure vanish through the door into the back room. Then she was climbing the stairs. Halfway up, her movements slowed as if she had been struck. Her mirror told the story of her punishment. The lean face of a woman of fifty-five met her stunned gaze. The disaster was complete. Cold, stiff, tearless, she waited for the police.

CHAPTER FIVE

For Garson, the world of the future began as a long dim corridor that he had a hard time keeping in focus with his unsteady vision. Heavy hands held him erect as he walked.

A wave of blur blotted out the uncertain picture.

When he could see again, the pressure of unpleasant hands was gone from him, and he was in a small room, sitting down. His first impression was that he was alone. Yet when he shook his head, and his vision cleared, he saw the desk; and behind the desk was a man.

The sight of that lean, dark, saturnine face sent a shock along his nerves, and swiftly galvanized a measure of strength back into his body. He leaned forward, his attention gathered on the man, and that was like a signal. Dr. Lell said derisively:

'I know. You've decided to co-operate. It was in your mind even before we left the presence of Norma, to whose rescue you came with such impetuous gallantry. Unfortunately, it isn't only a matter of making up *your* mind.'

The sneer in the man's voice made Garson uneasy. He thought, not coherently, not even chronologically: Lucky he was here in this room. Damned lucky they hadn't sprung a complication of futuristic newness on him, and so disorganized his concentration. Now there was time to gather his thoughts, harden his mind to every conceivable development, discount surprises, and *stay alive*.

He said, 'It's quite simple. You've got Norma. You've got me in your power, here in your own age. I'd be a fool to resist.'

Dr. Lell regarded him almost pityingly for a moment. But the sneer was in his tone again when he spoke. 'My dear Professor Garson, discussion at this point would be futile. My purpose is merely to discover if you are the type we can use in our laboratories. If you are not, the alternative is the de-personalizing chamber. I can say this much: men of your character type have not, on the average, been successful in passing our tests.'

Every word of that was like a penetrating, edged thing. In spite of his contempt, this man was indifferent to him. There

27

was only the test, whatever that was; and his own conscious life at stake. The important thing was to stay calm, and to continue to insist that he would cooperate. Before he could speak, Dr. Lell said in a curiously flat voice:

'We have a machine that tests human beings for degree of recalcitrancy. The Observer Machine will speak to you now!'

'What is your name?' said a voice out of the thin air beside Garson.

Garson jumped. He had a bad moment of mental unbalance. In spite of his determination, he had been caught off guard. Without his being aware of it, he had actually been in a state of extreme tension. With an effort he caught himself. He saw that Dr. Lell was smiling again, and that helped. Trembling, he leaned back in his chair; and, after a moment, he was sufficiently recovered to feel a surge of anger at the way the chill clung to his body, and at the tiny quaver in his voice as he began to answer:

'My name is John Bellmore Garson; age, thirty-three; research scientist; professor of physics at the University of – blood type number . . .'

There were too many questions, an exhaustive drain of detail out of his mind, the history of his life and aspirations. In the end, the truth was a cold weight inside him. His life, his awareness was at stake. Here was not comedy, but a precise, thorough, machinelike grilling. He must pass this test.

'Dr. Lell!' The insistent voice of the machine broke in. 'What is the state of this man's mind at this moment?'

Dr. Lell said promptly, 'Tremendous doubt. He is in a highly disturbed state.'

Garson drew a deep breath. He felt sick at the simple way he had been demoralized. And by one new thing. Here was a machine that needed neither telephone nor radio – if it was a machine. His voice was a rasping thing in his own ears as he snapped, 'My disturbed feeling can go straight to hell! I'm a reasonable person. I've made up my mind. I play ball with your organization to the limit.'

The silence that followed was unnaturally long; and when at last the machine spoke, his relief lasted only until its final words penetrated. The disembodied voice said, 'I am pessimistic, but bring him over for the test after the usual preliminaries.'

He began to feel better as he walked behind Dr. Lell along the gray-blue hallway. In a small way, he had won. Whatever these other tests were, how could they possibly ignore his determined conviction that he must co-operate?

It was more than just staying alive. For a man of his training this world of the future offered endless opportunities. Surely, he could resign himself to his lot for the duration of this war and concentrate on the amazing immensity of a science that included time portation, fireballs, and Observer Machines that judged men with a cold, remorseless logic and spoke out of the air. He frowned. There must be some trick to that, some 'telephone' in the nearby wall. Damned if he'd believe any force could focus sound without intermediary instruments, just as Norma couldn't have been made older that day in the police station without something mechanical.

The thought ended in a gasp of alarm. For a moment he stared, half paralyzed, down to where the floor had been. It wasn't there! Garson grabbed at the opaque wall; and then, as a low laugh came from the doctor, and the continued hardness beneath his feet told the extent of the illuson, he controlled himself, and stared in gathering fascination.

Below him was a section of a room whose limits he could not see because the opaque walls barred his vision on either side. A milling pack of men filled every available foot of space that he could see.

The ironic voice of Dr. Lell came to him, echoing his thoughts with brittle words. 'Men, yes, men! Recruits from all times. Soldiers-to-be from the ages, and not yet do they know their destiny.'

The voice ended, but the confusion below went on. Men squirmed, shoved, fought. Upturned faces showed puzzlement, anger, fear, amusement, and combinations of emotions. There were men in clothes that sparkled with every color of the rainbow; there were the drab-colored, the in-betweens; there were more than he could ever count.

Garson caught his flitting mind, and began to observe the scene more closely. In spite of the radical difference in the dress styles of the men who floundered down there like sheep in a slaughterhouse pen, there was a sameness about them that could only mean one thing.

'You're right!' It was that cool, taunting voice again. 'They're all Americans, all from this one city now called Delpa. From our several thousand machines located in the variuos ages of Delpa, we obtain about four thousand men an hour during the daylight hours. What you see below is the main receiving room. The recruits come sliding down the time chutes, and are promptly revived and shoved in there. Naturally, at this stage there is a certain amount of disorder. But let us proceed further.'

Garson scarcely noticed as the solid floor leaped into place beneath his feet. He did think that at no time had he seen Dr. Lell press a button or manipulate a control of any kind, neither when the Observer Machine spoke with ventriloquistic wizardry, nor when the floor was made invisible, nor when it again became opaque. Possibly here was some form of mental control. His mind leaped to a personal danger. What was the purpose of this preliminary? Were they showing him horror, then watching his reactions? He felt rage. What did they except from a man brought up in a twentieth century environment? Nothing here had anything to do with his intellectual conviction that he was caught and that therefore he must co-operate. But four thousand men in one hour from one city! He felt shocked and unhappy.

'And here,' said Dr. Lell, and his voice was as calm and placid as the water of a lily pond, 'we have one of several hundred smaller rooms that make a great circle around the primary time machine. You can see the confusion has diminished.'

It was an understatement, Garson thought. There was no confusion at all. Men sat on lounges and chairs. Some were looking at books. Others chatted like people in a silent movie: their lips moved, but no sound penetrated the illusive transparency of the floor.

'I didn't,' came that calm, smooth, confident voice, 'show you the intermediate stage that leads up to this clublike atmosphere. A thousand frightened men confronted with danger could make trouble. But we winnow them down, psychologically and physically, until we have one man going through that door at the end of the room – ah, there's one going now. Let us by all means follow hm. You see, at this point we dispense with coddling and bring forth the naked reality.'

The reality was a metal, boiler-shaped affair with a furnacelike door; and four beast humans simply grabbed the startled newcomer and thrust him feet first into the door.

The man must have screamed, for his face twisted upward, and the contorted fear, the almost idiotic gaping and working of the mouth, came at Garson like an enormous physical blow. As from a great distance, he heard Dr. Lell say, 'It helps at this stage to disorganize the patient's mind, for then the depersonalizing machine can do a better job.'

Abruptly, the indifference went out of his voice. In an icily curt tone, he said, 'It is useless to continue this little lecture tour. To my mind, your reactions have fully justified the pessimism of the Observer. There will be no further delay.'

The threat scarcely touched Garson. He was drained of emotion, of hope; and that first blaze of scientific eagerness was a dull ember. After that incredible succession of blows, he accepted the verdict of failure.

CHAPTER SIX

He came slowly out of that defeatist mood. Damn it, there was still the fact that he was committed to this world. He'd have to harden himself, narrow his emotions down to a channel that would include only Norma and himself. If these people and their machine condemned on the basis of feelings, then he'd have to show them how stony-cold his intellect could be. Where the devil was this all-knowing machine?

The corridor ended abruptly in a plain black door exactly like all the other doors. It held no promise of anything important beyond. The others had led to rooms and other corridors. This one opened onto a street.

A street of the city of the future!

Garson stiffened. His brain soared beyond contemplation of his own danger in a burning anticipation; and then, almost instantly, began to sag. Puzzled, he stared at a scene that was different from his expectations. In a vague way, mindful of the effects of war, he had pictured devastated magnificence. But it was not like that.

Before him stretched a depressingly narrow, unsightly street. Dark, unwashed buildings towered up to hide the sun. A trickle of the squat, semihuman men and women, beastlike creatures, moved stolidly along narrow areas of pavement marked off by black lines. That seemed to be the only method by which the road was distinguished from the sidewalk. The street stretched away into distance and it was all like that, as far as he could see. Intensely disappointed, conscious even of disgust, Garson turned away – and grew aware that Dr. Lell was staring at him with that grim smile.

The doctor said, 'What you are looking for, Professor Garson, you will not find, not in this or similar cities of the 'slaves,' but in the palace cities of the Glorious and the Planetarians –' He stopped, as if his words had brought an unpleasant thought. To Garson's amazement, his face twisted with rage. His voice was harsh as he spat, 'Those damnable Planetarians! When I think what their so-called ideals are bringing the world to, I –'

The fury passed. He went on quietly, 'Several hundred years ago, a mixed commission of Glorious and Planetarians surveyed the entire physical resources of the solar system. Men had made themselves practically immortal; theoretically, this body of mine will last a million years, barring major accidents. It was decided that available resources would maintain ten million men on Earth, ten million on Venus, five million on Mars, and ten million altogether on the moons of Jupiter for one million years at the then-existing high standard of consumption. Roughly, this would amount to about four million dollars a year per person by your standards of value, circa 1960.

'If in the meantime man conquered the stars, all these figures were subject to revision, though then, as now, the latter possibility was considered as remote as the stars themselves. Under examination, the problem of interstellar transport, apparently so simple, had shown itself intricate beyond the scope of our mathematics.'

He paused, and Garson ventured, 'We had versions of planned states too, but they always broke down because of human nature. That seems to have happened again.'

Garson did not think of the possibility of his statement being dangerous to him. The effect of his words was startling. The lean, handsome face became like frozen marble. Harshly, Dr. Lell said:

'Do not dare to compare your primitive societies to *us!* We are the rulers of all future time, and who in the past could ever stand against us if we chose to dominate? We shall win this war, in spite of being on the verge of defeat, for we are building the greatest time-energy barrier that has ever existed. With it, we shall ensure that we win – or no one will win! We'll teach those moralistic scum of the planets to prate about man's rights and freedom of the spirit. Blast them all!'

He spoke with violent emotion. But Garson did not back down. He had his opinions, and it was clear that he could not hope to conceal them from either Dr. Lell or the Observer, so he said:

'I see an aristocrat hierarchy and a swarm of beastmen slaves. How do *they* fit into the picture, anyway? What about the resources they require? There certainly seem to be hundreds of thousands in this city alone.'

The man was staring at him in rigid hostility. Garson felt a sudden chill. He hadn't expected that any reasonable statement he might make would be used against him. Dr. Lell said, too quietly, 'Basically, they do not use any resources. They live in cities of stone and brick, and eat the produce of the indefatigable soil.'

His voice was suddenly sharp as steel. 'And now, Professor Garson, I assure you that you have already condemned yourself. The Observer is located in that metal building across the street because the impact of energy from the great primary time machine would affect its sensitive parts if it were nearer. I can think of no other explanation that you require, and I certainly have no desire to remain in the company of a man who will be an automaton in half an hour. *Come along!*'

Garson did not argue. He was aware again of this monstrous city, and he thought bleakly, It's the same old, old story of the aristocrat justifying his black crime against his fellow man. Originally, there must have been deliberate physical degradation, deliberate misuse of psychology. The very name by which these people called themselves, the Glorious, seemed a heritage from days when enormous efforts must have been made to arouse hero worship in the masses.

Dr. Lell's dry voice said, 'Your disapproval of our slaves is shared by the Planetarians. They also oppose our methods of depersonalizing our recruits. It is easy to see that they and you have many things in common, and if only you could escape to their side . . .'

With an effort, Garson pulled himself out of his private world. He was being led on, not skillfully. It was apparent now that every word Dr. Lell spoke had the purpose of making him reveal himself. For a moment, he was conscious of impatience; then puzzlement came. 'I don't get it,' he said. 'What you're doing cannot be bringing forth any new facts. I'm the product of my environment. You know what that environment is, and what type of normal human being it must inevitably produce. As I've said, my whole case rests on co-operation.'

A difference in the color of the sky at the remote end of the street snatched his attention. It was a faint, abnormal, scarlet tinge like a mist, an unnatural, unearthly sunset, only it was hours yet before the sun would set. He felt himself growing taut. He said in a tense voice, 'What's that?'

'That,' Dr. Lell's curt, amused voice came at him, 'is the war.'

Garson laughed. He couldn't help it. For weeks, speculation about this gigantic war of the future had intertwined with his gathering anxiety about Norma. And now this red haze on the horizon of an otherwise undamaged city – the war!

The dark flash of laughter ended as Dr. Lell said, 'It is not as amusing as you think. Most of Delpa is intact because it is protected by a local time-energy barrier. Delpa is actually under siege, fifty miles inside enemy territory.' He must have caught the thought that came to Garson. He said good-humoredly, 'You're right. All you have to do is get out of Delpa, and you'll be safe.'

Garson said angrily, 'It's a thought that would occur to any intelligent person. Don't forget you have Miss Matheson.'

Dr. Lell seemed not to have heard. 'The red haze you see is the point where the enemy has neutralized our energy barrier. It is there that they attack us unceasingly day and night with an inexhaustible store of robot machines.

'We are unfortunate in not having the factory capacity in Delpa to build robot weapons, so we use a similar type manned by depersonalized humans. Unfortunately, again, the cost in lives is high; one hundred percent of recruits. Every day, too, we lose about forty feet of city, and, of course, in the end Delpa will fall.' He smiled, an almost gentle smile. Garson was amazed to notice that he seemed suddenly in high good humor as he said, 'You can see how effective even a small time-energy barrier is. When we complete the great barrier two years hence, our entire front line will be literally impregnable.

'As for your co-operation argument, it's worthless. Men are braver than they think, braver than reason. But let's forget argument. In a minute, the machine will give us the truth of this matter.'

CHAPTER SEVEN

At first sight, the Observer Machine was a solid bank of flickering lights that steadied as they surveyed him. Garson waited under that many-faceted gaze, scarcely breathing. He didn't think that the wall of black metal machine and lights was very impressive, and found himself analyzing the lack. It was too big and too stationary. If it had been small and possessed of shape, however ugly, and *movement*, there might have been a suggestion of abnormal personality. Here were a myriad lights on a metal wall. As he watched, the lights began to wink again. Abruptly, they blinked out, all except a little colored design of them at the bottom right-hand corner.

Behind Garson, the door opened, and Dr. Lell came into the silent room. 'I'm glad,' he said quietly, 'that the result was what it was. We are desperately in need of good assistants. To illustrate,' he went on as they emerged into the brightness of the unpleasant street, 'I am, for instance, in charge of that recruiting station in the twentieth century, but I'm there only when an inter-time alarm system has warned me. In the interim, I am employed on scientific duties of the second order – first order being work which, by its very nature, must continue without interruption.'

They were back at the same great building from which they had come, and ahead stretched the same gray-blue, familiar corridor, only this time Dr. Lell opened the first of several doors. He bowed politely. 'After you, Professor.'

A fraction too late, Garson's fist flailed the air where that dark, strong face had been. They stared at each other, Garson tight-lipped, his brain like a steel bar. The superman said softly:

'You will always be that instant too slow, Professor. It is a lack you cannot remedy. You know, of course, that my little speech was designed to keep you quiet during the trip back here, and actually you failed the test. What you do not know is that you failed startlingly, with a recalcitrancy grading of six, which is the very worst, and intelligence AA plus, almost the very best. It is too bad because we really need capable assistants. I regret –'

36

'Let me do the regretting!' Garson cut him off roughly. 'If I remember rightly, it was just below here that your beast men were forcing a man into the depersonalizing machine. Perhaps, on the staircase going down, I can find some way of tripping you up, and knocking that little gun you're palming right out of your hand.'

There was something in the smile of the other that should have warned him, a hint of sly amusement. Not that it would have made any difference. He stepped warily through the open doorway and headed toward the gray-blue, plainly visible stairway. Behind him, the door clicked with an odd finality.

Ahead, the staircase was gone – a vanished illusion. Where it had been was a large boilerlike case with a furnace-shaped door. Half a dozen beast men came forward. A moment later they were shoving him toward that black hole of a door.

The second day, Norma took the risk. The windows of the recruiting station still showed the same blank interior; walls stripped by the police of Calonian slogans, and signs and newspaper clippings trampled all over the floor. The door of the back room was half closed, and it was too dark to see the interior.

It was noon. With drummed-up courage, Norma walked swiftly to the front entrance. The lock clicked open smoothly. She stepped inside and a moment later was pushing at the back door. The machine was not there. Great dents showed in the floor where it had stood for so many months. But it was gone as completely as Dr. Lell, as completely as the beast men and Jack Garson.

Back in her rooms, she collapsed onto the bed, and lay quivering from the dreadful nervous reaction of that swift, illegal search.

On the afternoon of the fourth day, as she sat staring at the meaningless words of a book, there was an abrupt tingling in her body. Somewhere a machine – *the machine* – was vibrating softly. She climbed to her feet, the book forgotten on the window sill where, freakishly, it had fallen. But the sound was gone. Not a tremor touched her taut nerves. The thought came: Imagination! Her tension was really beginning to affect her.

As she stood there, stiff, unable to relax, there came the thin squeal of a door opening downstairs. It was the back door that led into the vacant lot which her window over-looked. The back door opening and shutting! As she watched, fascinated, Dr. Lell stalked into view. Her awareness of him was so sharp that he must have caught it, but he did not turn. In half a minute he was gone, out of her vision.

On the fifth day, there was hammering downstairs, carpenters working. Several trucks came, and she heard the mumbling sound of men talking. But it was evening before she dared venture down. Through the window, then, she saw the beginning of the changes that were being wrought. The old bench had been removed. The walls were being redone. There was no new furniture yet, but a rough, unfinished sign leaned against the wall. It read: EMPLOYMENT BUREAU — MEN WANTED.

Men wanted! So that was it. Another trap for men! Those ravenous armies of the future must be kept glutted with fodder. The incredible war in that incredible future raged on.

She watched dumbly as Dr. Lell came out of the back room. He walked toward the front door, and she waited helplessly as he opened the door, looked in, and meticulously closed the door again. Then, a moment later, he stood beside her, as silent as she, also staring into the window. Finally, he said:

'I see you've been admiring our new set-up.'

His voice was matter-of-fact, and lacking in menace. She made no reply. He seemed to expect none, for he said almost immediately, in that same controversial tone, 'It's just as well that it all happened as it did. Nothing I ever told you has been disproved. I said that investigation had shown the machine to be here several years hence. Naturally, we could not examine every day or week of that time. This little episode accordingly escaped our notice, but did not change the situation.

'As for the fact that it will be an employment bureau henceforth, that seemed natural at the period of our investigation because this Calonian War was over then.'

He paused, and still there was no word that she could think to say. In gathering darkness, he seemed to stare at her. He said, 'I'm telling you all this because it would be annoying to have to train someone else for your position, and because you must realize the impossibility of further opposition. Accept your situation. We have thousands of machines similar to this, and the millions of men flowing

38

through them are gradually turning the tide of battle in our favor. We must win; our cause is overwhelmingly just. We are Earth against all the planets; Earth protecting herself against the aggression of a combination of enemies armed as no powers in all time have ever been armed. We have the highest moral right to draw on the men of Earth of every century to defend their planet.

'However' – his voice lost its objectivity, grew colder – 'if this logic does not move you, the following rewards for your good behaviour should prove efficacious. We have Professor Garson. Unfortunately, I was unable to save his personality. Definite tests proved that he would be a recalcitrant. But there is your youth. It will be returned to you on a salary basis. Every three weeks you will become a year younger. In short, it will require two years for you to return to your version of twenty.'

He finished on a note of command. 'A week from today, this bureau will open for business. You will report at nine o'clock. This is your last chance. Good-by.'

In the darkness, she watched his shape turn. He vanished into the gloom of the building.

She had a purpose. At first it was a tiny mind-growth that she wouldn't admit into her consciousness. But gradually embarrassment passed, and the whole world of her thought began to organize around it.

It began with the developing realization that resistance was useless. Not that she believed in the rightness of the cause of this race that called itself the Glorious, although his story of Earth against the planets had put the first doubt into her brain. As, she knew, he had intended it should. The affair was simpler than that. One woman had set herself against the men of the future. What a silly thing for one to do!

But there remained Jack Garson . . .

If she could get him back – poor, broken, strange creature that he must be now with his personality destroyed – somehow she would make amends for having been responsible. She thought: What madness to hope that they'd give him back to her, ever! She was the tiniest cog in a vast war machine. Nevertheless, the fact remained. She must get him back!

The part of her brain that was educated, civilized, thought: What an elemental purpose, everything drained out of her but the basics, one woman concentrating on one man.

But the purpose was there, unquenchable.

The slow months dragged, and once gone, seemed to have flashed by. One night she turned a corner and found herself on a street she hadn't visited for some time. She stopped short, her body stiffening. The street ahead was swarming with men but their presence scarcely touched her mind.

Above all that confusion of sound, above the catcalls, above the roar of streetcars and automobiles, above the totality of the cacophonous combination, there was another sound, an incredibly softer sound – the whisper of a time machine. She was miles from the employment bureau with its machine, but the tiny tremor along her nerves was un-mistakable.

She pressed forward, blind to everything but the attention of the men. A man tried to put his arm through hers. She jerked free automatically. Another man simply caught her in an embrace, and for brief seconds she was subjected to a hard hug and a hard kiss. Purpose gave her strength. With scarcely an effort, she freed one arm and struck at his face. The man laughed good-humoredly, released her, but walked beside her. 'Clear the way for the lady!' he shouted.

Almost magically, there was a lane; and she was at the window. There was a sign that read:

WANTED
RETURNED SOLDIERS
FOR DANGEROUS ADVENTURE
GOOD PAY!

She felt no emotion as she realized that here was another trap for men. In her brain she had space for only an impres-sion. The impression was of a large square room, with a dozen men in it. Only three of the men were recruits. Of the other nine, one was an American soldier dressed in the uni-form of World War I. He sat at a desk pounding a type-writer. Over him leaned a Roman legionnaire of the time of Julius Caesar, complete with toga and short sword. Beside the door, holding back the pressing throng of men, were two Greek soldiers of the time of Pericles.

The men and the times they represented were unmistak-able to her, who had taken four college years of Latin and

Greek and acted in plays of both periods in the original languages. There was another man in an ancient costume, but she was unable to place him. At the moment, he was at a short counter interviewing one of the three recruits. Of the four remaining men, two wore uniforms that could have been developments of the late twentieth century. The cloth was of a light-yellowish color, and both men had two pips on their shoulders. The rank of lieutenant was obviously still in style when they were commissioned.

The remaining two men were simply strange, not in face, but in the cloth of their uniforms. Their faces were of sensitive, normal construction. Their uniforms consisted of breeches and neatly fitting coats all in blue, a blue that sparkled as from a million needlelike diamond points. In a quiet, blue, intense way, they shone.

As she watched, one of the recruits was led to the back door. It was her first awareness that there was a back door. The door opened; she had the briefest glimpse of a towering machine and a flashing picture of a man who was tall and dark of face, and who might have been Dr. Lell. Only he wasn't. But the similarity of race was unmistakable.

The door closed, and one of the Greeks guarding the outer entrance said, 'All right, two more of you fellows can come in.'

There was a struggle for position, brief but violent. And then the two victors, grinning and breathing heavily from their exertion, were inside. In the silence that followed, one of the Greeks turned to the other, and said in a tangy, almost incomprehensible version of ancient Greek :

'Sparta herself never had more willing fighters. This promises to be a good night's catch.'

It was the rhythm of the words, and the colloquial gusto with which they were spoken, that almost destroyed the meaning for her. After a moment, however, she made the mental translation. And now the truth was clear. The men of Time had gone back even to old Greece, probably much further back, for their recruits. And always they had used every version of bait, based on all the weaknesses and urgencies in the natures of man.

Fight for Calonia! – an appeal to idealism. *Men Wanted!* – the most basic of all appeals, work for food, happiness, security. And now, the appeal variation was for returned soldiers – *Adventure With Pay!*

41

Diabolical! And yet so effective that they could use as recruiting officers men who had been caught by the same propaganda. These men must be of the non-recalcitrant type, who fitted themselves willingly into the war machine of the Glorious. Traitors! Abruptly ablaze with hatred for all non-recalcitrants who still possessed their personalities, she whirled away from the window.

She was thinking : Thousands of such machines. The figures had been meaningless before, but now, with just one other machine as a measurable example, the reality reared up into a monstrous thing. To think that there had been a time when she had actually set herself, singlehanded, against *them*.

There remained the problem of getting Jack Garson out of the hell of that titanic war of the future!

At night she walked the streets, because there was always the fear that in the apartment her thoughts, her driving, deadly thoughts, would be tapped. And because to be enclosed in those narrow walls above the machine that had devoured so many thousands of men was intolerable. She thought as she walked, over and over she thought of the letter Jack Garson had written her before he came in person. The letter was long destroyed, but every word was recorded on her brain. And of all the words in it, the one sentence that she kept returning to was : *In your position, I would ask myself one question : Was there anything, any metal, anything upon my person that might have been placed there?*

One day, as she was wearily unlocking the door of her apartment, the answer came. Perhaps it was the extra weariness that brought her briefly closer to basic things. Perhaps her brain was simply tired of slipping over the same blind spot. Or perhaps the months of concentration had finally earned the long-delayed result. Whatever the reason, she was putting the key back into her purse when the hard, metallic feel of it against her fingers brought realization.

The key was metal! The key –

Desperately, she stopped the repetition. The apartment door slammed behind her, and like some terrorized creature she fled down the dark stairs into the glare of the night streets. Impossible to return until she had answered the burning question in her mind. Until she had made sure!

After half an hour, a measure of coherence came. In a drugstore, she bought an overnight case and a few fill-ins to

42

give it weight. A pair of small pliers, a pair of tweezers – in case the pliers were too large – and a small screwdriver completed her equipment. Then she went to a hotel.

The pliers and the tweezers were all she needed. The little bulbous cap of the skeleton-type key yielded to the first hard pressure. Her trembling fingers completed the unscrewing – and she found herself staring at a tiny, glowing point, like a red-hot needle protruding from the very center of the tube that was inside the key. The needle was absorbed into an intricate design of spiderlike wires, all visible in the glow that emanated from them.

She thought uncertainly that here were probably terrific energies. She was not restrained by the possibility. But enough of the reality of the danger stayed with her to make her wrap her flimsy lace handkerchief around the tweezers. Then she touched the shining, protruding needle point. It yielded the slightest bit to her shaky touch. Nothing happened. It continued to glow.

Dissatisfied, she put the key down and stared at it. So tiny, so delicate a machine actually disturbed to the extent of one-sixteenth of an inch displacement. And nothing happened. A sudden thought sent her to the mirror. A forty-year-old face stared back at her.

It was months since she had returned to twenty. And now, in a flash, she was forty. The touch of the tweezers against the needle's end, pushing, had aged her twenty years.

That explained what had happened at the police station. It meant that if she could only pull it back . . . She fought to steady her fingers, then applied the tweezers.

She was twenty again!

Abruptly weak, she lay down on the bed. She thought: Somewhere in the world of time and space was the still-living body of the man that had been Jack Garson. But for him she could throw this key thing into the river three blocks away, take the first train east or west or south, and the power of the machine would be futile against her. Dr. Lell would not seriously consider searching for her once she had lost herself in the swarm of humankind.

How simple it all was, really. For three long years, their power over her had been the key and its one devastating ability to age her. Or was that all? Startled, she sat up. Did they count, perhaps, on victims believing themselves safe enough to keep the key and its magic powers of rejuvenation. She,

43

of course, because of Jack Garson, was bound to the key as if it were still the controller, and not she. But the other incentive, now that she had thought of it, was enormous.

Her fingers shook as she picked up the key with its glowing, intricate interior. It seemed incredible that they could have allowed the precious instrument to pass so easily into the hands of an alien, when they must have known that there was a probability of discovery.

She had an idea then; she grew calm. With suddenly steady fingers, she picked up the tweezers, caught the protruding glow point of the key between the metal jaws and, making no attempt to pull or push, twisted clockwise. There was a tiny, almost inaudible click. Her body twanged like a taut violin string, and then she was falling, falling into dark, immense distance.

Out of that night, a vaguely shining body drifted toward her, a body human yet not human. There was something about the head and the shoulders, something physically different, that eluded her slow thought. And in that strange, superhuman head were eyes that blazed like jewels, and seemed literally to pierce her. The voice that came couldn't have been sound, for it was inside her brain, and it said:

'With this great moment, you enter upon your power and your purpose. I say to you, the time-energy barrier must not be completed. It will destroy all ages of the solar system. The time-energy barrier must *not* be completed!'

The body faded, and was gone. The very memory of it became a dim mind-shape. There remained the darkness, the jet-black incredible darkness.

Abruptly, she was in a material world. She seemed to be half-slumped, half-kneeling, one leg folded under her in the exact position she had occupied on the bed. Only she must have drooped there unconscious for long moments. Her knees ached with the hard, pressing pain of her position. And, beneath the silk of her stockings was, not the hotel bed, but metal!

CHAPTER EIGHT

It was the combination of surprise, the aloneness, and the stark fact of what was happening that unnerved Garson. He started to squirm, then he was writhing, his face twisted in agony. And then the strength of the rough, stolid hands holding him seemed to flow somehow along his nerves.

He willed himself calm. And was safe from madness!

There were no hands touching him now. He lay, face downward, on a flat hard surface; and at first there was only the darkness and a slow return of the sense of aloneness. Vague thoughts came, thoughts of Norma and the coincidence that had molded his life, seemingly so free for so many years, yet destined to find its ending here in this black execution chamber. For he was being destroyed here, though his body might live on for a few brief mindless hours. Or days. Or weeks. The time didn't matter.

The thing was fantastic. Surely, in a minute he'd wake up from this nightmare.

At first the sound was less than a whisper, a stealthy noise out of remoteness, that prodded with an odd insistence at Garson's hearing. It quivered toward him in the blackness, a rasping presence that grew louder – voices! It exploded into a monstrous existence, a billion voices clamoring at his brain, a massive blare that pressed at him. Abruptly, the ferocity of the voices dimmed. They faded into the distance, still insistent, somehow reluctant to leave, as if there was something still left unsaid.

The end of sound came, and, briefly, there was utter silence. Then there was a click. Light flooded at him from an opening a scant foot from his head. Garson twisted and stared, fascinated. Daylight! From his vantage point, he could see the edge of a brick-and-stone building, a wretchedly old, worn building, a street of Delpa.

It was over. Incredibly, it was over. And nothing had happened. No, that wasn't it exactly. There were things in his mind, confusing things about the importance of loyalty to the Glorious, a sense of intimacy with his surroundings, pictures of machines, but nothing clear.

A harsh voice broke his amazed blur of thought. 'Come on out of there, you damned slowpoke!'

A square, heavy, brutal face was peering into the open door. The face belonged to a big, square-built young man with a thick neck, a boxer's flat nose, and unpleasant blue eyes.

Garson lay quite still. It was not that he intended to disobey. His reason urged instant, automatic obedience until he could estimate the astounding things that had happened. What held him there, every muscle stiff, was a new, tremendous fact that grew, not out of the meaning of the man's words, but out of the words themselves.

The language was not English. Yet he understood every word.

The sudden squint of impatient rage that flushed the coarse face peering in at him brought life to Garson's muscles. He scrambled forward, but it was the man's big hands that actually pulled him clear and deposited him with a jarring casualness face downward on the paved road.

He lay tense for an instant, fighting mad. Yet he dare not show his anger. Something had gone wrong. The machine hadn't worked all the way, and he must not wreck the great chance that offered. He stood up slowly, wondering how an automaton, a depersonalized human being, should look and act.

'This way, damn you,' said the bullying voice from behind him. 'You're in the army now.' Satisfaction came into the voice. 'Well, you're the last for me today. I'll get you fellows to the front, and then –'

'This way' led to a dispirited-looking group of men, about a hundred of them, who stood in two rows alongside a great, gloomy, dirty building. Garson walked stolidly to the end of the rear line, and for the first time realized how surprisingly straight the formation of men were holding their lines, in spite of dulled appearance.

'All right, all right,' bellowed the square-jawed young man. 'Let's get going. You've got some hard fighting ahead of you before this day and night are over.'

It struck Garson, as he stared at the leader, that this was the type they picked for nonrecalcitrant training: the ignorant, blatant, amoral, sensual pigman type. No wonder he himself had been rejected by the Observer. His eyes narrowed to slits as he watched the line of dead-alive men walk by

46

him in perfect rhythm. He fell in step, his mind deliberately slow and ice-cold. Cautiously he explored the strange knowledge in his brain that didn't fit with his freedom.

It didn't, in fact, fit with anything that had happened. But it was there, nevertheless, a little group of sentences that kept repeating inside him : *The great time-energy barrier is being built in Delpa. It must not be completed, for it will destroy the universe. Prepare to do your part in its destruction. Try to tell the Planetarians, but take no unnecessary risks. To stay alive, to tell the Planetarians, those are your immediate purposes. The time-energy barrier must not – not –'*

The repetition grew monotonous. He squeezed the crazy thing out of his consciousness.

No trucks came gliding along to transport them, no streetcar whispered along in some futuristic development of street-railway service. There was no machinery, nothing but those narrow avenues with their gray, sidewalkless lengths, like back alleys.

They walked to war; and it was like being in an old, dead, deserted city. Deserted except for the straggle of short, thick, slow, stolid men and women who plodded heavily by, unsmiling and without a side glance. As if they were but the pitiful, primitive remnants of a once-great race, and this city the proud monument to – *no!* Garson smiled wryly. It was foolish to feel romantic about this monstrosity of a city. Even without Dr. Lell's words as a reminder, it was evident that every narrow, dirty street, and every squalid building had been erected to be what it was.

And the sooner he got out of the place, and delivered to the Planetarians the queer, inexplicable message about the great time-energy barrier, the better off he'd be. With deliberate abruptness, he cut the thought. He'd have to be careful. If one of the Glorious should happen to be around, and accidently catch the free thought of what was supposed to be an automaton, next time there'd be no mistake.

Tramp, tramp, tramp! The pavement echoed hollowly, like a ghost city. He had the tremendous thought that he was here centuries, perhaps millennia, into the future. What an awful realization to think that Norma, poor, persecuted, enslaved Norma, whose despairing face he had seen little more than an hour ago, was actually dead and buried in the dim ages of the long ago. And yet she was alive. Those six hundred billion bodies per minute of hers were somewhere in

47

space and time, alive because the great time-energy cycle followed its casual, cosmic course of endless repetition, because life was but an accident as purposeless as the immeasurable energy that plunged grandly on into the unknown night. Tramp, tramp, on and on, and this thought was a rhythm to the march.

At last he came out of his reverie, and saw the red haze in the near distance ahead. It wouldn't take ten minutes more, and they'd be *there!* Machines glinted in the slanting rays of the warm, golden, sinking sun; machines that moved and fought! A sick thrill struck Garson, the first shock of realization that this tiny segment of the battle of the ages was real, and near, and deadly. Up there, men were dying every minute, dying miserably for a cause their depersonalized minds did not even comprehend. Up there, too, was infinitesimal victory for the Planetarians, and a small, stinging measure of defeat for the Glorious. Forty feet a day, Dr. Lell had said.

Forty feet of city conquered every day. What a murderous war of attrition. What a bankruptcy of strategy. Or was it the ultimate nullification of the role of military genius, in that each side knew and practised every rule of military science without error? If so, then the forty feet was simply the inevitable mathematical outcome of the difference in the potential in striking power of the two forces.

Forty feet a day. Wonderingly, Garson stood finally with his troop a hundred yards from that unnatural battlefront. Like a robot he stood stiffly among those robot men, but his eyes and mind fed in undiminished fascination at the deadly mechanical routine that was the offense and defense.

In the limited area that he could see, the Planetarians had seven major machines, and there were at least half a hundred tiny, swift, glittering craft as escort for each of the great — *battleships*. That was it: battleships and destroyers! Against them, the Glorious had only destroyers, a host of darting, shining, torpedo-shaped craft that hugged the ground and fought in an endlessly repeated complicated maneuver. He could guess that similar battles progressed for a hundred miles all around them.

Maneuver against maneuver; an intricate game, whose purpose and method seemed to quiver just beyond the reach of his reason. Everything revolved around the battleships. In some way they must be protected from energy guns, because

48

no attempt was made to use energy against them. Somehow, too, cannon must be useless against them. There was none in sight, nor was there any other method of propelling solid objects at the machines. The Planetarians did not even fire at the more than a hundred troops like his own, who stood at stiff attention so close to the front, so bunched that a few superexplosive shells of the past would have smashed them all. There was nothing but the battleships and the destroyers!

The battleships moved forward and backward and forward and backward and in and out, intertwining among themselves; and the destroyers of the Glorious darted in when the battleships came forward, and hung back when the battleships retreated. And always the destroyers of the Planetarians were gliding in to intercept the destroyers of the Glorious. As the sun sank in a blaze of red beyond the green hills to the west, the battleships in their farthest forward thrust were feet closer than they had been at the beginning; and the sharply delineated red line of haze, which must be the point where the time-energy barrier was neutralized, was no longer lying athwart a shattered slab of rock, but on the ground feet nearer.

That was it. The battleships somehow forced the time-energy barrier to be withdrawn. Obviously, it would only be withdrawn to save it from a worse fate, perhaps from a complete neutralization over a wide front. And so a city was being won, inch by inch, foot by foot, street by street. Only the intricate evolution of the battle, the way of that almost immeasurably slow victory, was as great a mystery as ever.

Garson thought grimly: If the message that had come into his brain in that out-of-order depersonalizing machine was true, then the final victory would not come quickly enough. Long before the forty-feet-a-day conquerors had gained the prize that was Delpa, the secret, super time-energy barrier would be completed, and the human race and all its works would be eliminated from the universe.

Night fell, but a glare of searchlights replaced the sun, and that fantastic battle raged on. No one aimed a gun or a weapon at the lights. Each side concentrated on its part of the intricate, murderous game, and troop after troop dissolved into the ravenous, incredible conflagration.

Death came simply to the automatons. Each in turn crowded into one of the torpedo-shaped destroyers. Each individual had learned from the depersonalizing machine that the tiny, man-sized tank was operated by thought control. Highly trained in that limited sense, the human automaton flashed out to the battleline. Sometimes the end came swiftly, sometimes it was delayed, but sooner or later there was a metallic contact with the enemy, and that was all that the enemy needed. Instantly, the machine would twist and race toward the line of waiting men; the next victim would drag out the corpse and crawl in himself.

There were variations. Machines clashed with the enemy and died with their drivers, or darted aimlessly out of control. Always, swift metallic scavengers raced from both sides to capture the prize; and sometimes the Planetarians succeeded, sometimes the Glorious. Garson counted: one two, three – less than four hundred men ahead of him. As he realized how close his turn was, cold perspiration beaded his face. Minutes, *damn it!* He had to solve the rules of this battle, or go in there without a plan, without hope.

Seven battleships, scores of destroyers to each battleship and all acting as one unit in one involved maneuver.

And, by heaven, he had a part of the answer. One unit. Not seven battleships out there, but one in the form of seven. One superneutralizing machine in its seven-dimensional maneuver. No wonder he had been unable to follow the intertwinings of those monsters with each other, the retreats, the advances. Mathematicians of the twentieth century could only solve easily problems with four equations. Here was a problem with seven, and the general staff of the Glorious could never be anything but a step behind in their solution. That step cost them forty feet a day.

It was his turn! He crept into the casing of the torpedo cycle, and it was smaller even than he had thought. The machine fitted him almost like a glove. Effortlessly, under his direction, it glided forward, too smoothly, too willingly, into that dazzle of searchlights, into that maelstrom of machines. One contact, he thought, one contact with an enemy meant death; and his plan of breaking through was as vague as his understanding of how a seven-dimensional maneuver actually worked.

Amazed wonder came that he was even letting himself hope.

CHAPTER NINE

Norma began to notice the difference, a strange, vibrant, quality within herself. She felt warmly alive, a new kind of aliveness added now to the life that had always existed within her.

Physically, she was still crouching there, her legs twisted under her, vision still blinded; and the hard pain of the metal beneath her was an unchanged pressure against the bone and muscle of her knees. But along every nerve crept that wonderful sense of wellbeing, of buoyant power. It yielded abruptly to the violence of the thought that flashed into her mind: *Where was she? What had happened? What —*

The thought ended as an alienness intruded into it, another thought, not out of her own mind, not even directed at her, not human!

Tentacle 2731 reporting to the Observer. A warning light has flashed on the ... (meaningless) ... time machine. Action!

The answer came instantly, coldly: *An intruder — on top of the primary time machine. Warning from, and to, Dr. Lell's section. Tentacle 2731, go at once — destroy intruder. Action!*

There was stunning significance in those hard wisps of message and answering message, that echoed back along the corridors of her mind. The stupefying fact that she had effortlessly intercepted thought waves momentarily blotted out the immediacy of the danger. The impact of the death threat struck her suddenly.

Before that menace, even the knowledge of where she was came with a quiet unobtrusiveness, like a minor harmony in a clash of major discord. Her present location was only too obvious. By twisting the key, she had been hurtled through time to the age of the Glorious, to the primary time machine, where fantastic things called tentacles and observers were ceaselessly on guard.

If only she could see! She *must* see, or she was lost before she could begin to hope. Frantically, she strained against the blackness that lay so tight against her eyes.

She saw!

It was simple as that. One instant, blindness. The next, the urge to see. And then, complete sight, without preliminary blue, like opening her eyes after a quiet sleep.

The simplicity of it was crowded out of her mind by a swirling confusion of impression. There were two swift thoughts that clung – a brief wonder at the way sight had come back to her, merely from that wish that it would, and a flashing memory of the face that had floated at her out of the blackness of time : *With this great moment you enter upon your power and your purpose!*

The picture, all connecting thoughts, fled. She saw that she was in a vast, domed room, and that she was on top of a gigantic machine. There were transparent walls. Through them, she saw a shimmering roseate fire, like a greater dome that covered the near sky and hid the night universe beyond.

The effort of staring tired her. Her gaze came down out of the sky; and back in the room, she saw that all the transparent wall that faced her was broken into a senseless pattern of small balconies, each mounting glittering, strangely menacing machinery : weapons! So many weapons, for what?

With a jar that shocked her brain, the thought disintegrated. She stared in horror at a long, thick, tube-shaped metal thing that floated up from below the rim of the time machine. A score of gleaming, insectlike facets seemed to glare at her.

Tentacle 2371 – destroy the intruder!

No! It was her own desperate negation, product of pure panic. All the bravery that had made her experiment with the key in the first place collapsed before the hideous alien threat. Her mind spun. She shrank from the terrible fear that this metal would spray her with some incredible flame weapon before she could think, before she could turn to run, or even move!

Of all her pride and accumulated courage, there remained only enough to bring a spasm of shame at the words that burst senselessly from her lips. 'No, no, you can't! Go away! Go back where you came from! Go! –'

She stopped, blinked, and stared wildly. The thing was gone!

The reality of that had scarcely touched her before a crash

sounded. It came from beyond and below the rim of the machine. Instinctively, Norma ran forward to peer down. The hundred foot, precipicelike slope of metal time-machine that greeted her startled gaze made her draw back with a gasp. But quickly she was creeping forward again, more cautiously, but with utter fascination to see once more what that first brief glimpse had revealed.

And there it was, on the distant floor, the tube-shaped thing. Even as she watched, hope building up in her, there came a weak impulse of alien thought:

Tentacle 2731 reporting – difficulty. Female human using Insel mind rays, power 100. No further action possible by this unit, incapacitation 74 mechanical –'

But I did say that, she thought incredulously. Her wish had brought instant return of sight. Her despairing thought had sent the tentacle crashing to mechanical ruin. Insel mind rays, power 100! Why, it meant – it could mean –

The leaping thought sagged. One of a series of doors in the wall facing her opened, and a tall man emerged hurriedly. She pressed back flat on the metal, out of sight; but it seemed to her *those familiar, sardonic eyes were staring straight up* at her. Dr. Lell's hard, superbly confident thought came then like a succession of battering blows against the crumbling structure of her hope:

This is a repetition of the X time and space manipulation. Fortunately, the transformation center this seventeenth time is a Miss Norma Matheson, who is incapable, mathematically, of using the power at her disposal. She must be kept confused. The solution to her swift destruction is a concentration of forces of the third order, nonmechanical, according to Plan A-4. Action!

Action immediate! came the cold, distinctive thought of the Observer.

That was like death itself. She abandoned hope, and lay flat on that flat metal, her mind blank and no strength in her body.

A minute passed and that seemed an immense time. So much that the swift form of her thought changed and hardened. Fear faded like a dream, and then she had a returning awareness of that curious, wonderful sense of power. She stood up, and the way her legs trembled with the effort brought the automatic memory of the way she had regained her vision. She thought tensely: *No more physical weakness.*

Every muscle, every nerve, every organ of my body must function perfectly from now on and –

A queer thrill cut the thought. It seemed to start at her toes, and sweep up, a delicious sense of warmth, like an all-over blush. And the weakness was gone.

She stood for a moment, fascinated. She hesitated to try the power too far. Yet the enormous threat stiffened her will. She thought: *No more mental weakness, no confusion; my brain must function with all the logic of which I am capable!*

What happened then was not altogether satisfactory. Her mind seemed to stop. For an instant the blankness was complete. And then a single, simple idea came into it: Danger! For her there was nothing but danger, and escape from that danger. Find the key. Go back. Get out of this world of Dr. Lell, and gain time to solve the secrets of the mighty power centralized in her.

She jerked as a lean, yard-long flame struck the metal beside her, and caromed away toward the ceiling. She watched it bounce from the ceiling, out of sight beyond the edge of the machine. It must have struck the floor, but instantly it was in sight again, leaping toward the ceiling with undiminished power. Up, down, up, down, up it went as she watched. Then, abruptly, it lost momentum and collapsed like an empty flaming sack toward the floor, out of her line of vision.

A second streamer of flame soared up from where Dr. Lell had been heading when last she saw him. It struck the ceiling and, like an elongated billiard ball, darted down – and this time she was ready for it. Her brain reached out: *Stop! Whatever the energy that drives you, it is powerless against me. Stop!*

The flame missed her right hand by inches, and soared on up to the ceiling; and from below, strong and clear and satirical, came the voice of Dr. Lell:

'My dear Miss Matheson, that's the first of the third order energies, quite beyond your control. And if you'll notice, your mind isn't as cool as you ordered it to be. The truth is that, although you have power unlimited, you can only use it when you understand the forces involved, either conscious- or unconsciously. Most people have a reasonably clear picture of their bodily processes, which is why your body reacted so favorably, but your brain – its secrets are largely beyond your understanding. As for the key' – there was

54

laughter in the words – 'you seem to have forgotten it is geared to the time machine. The Observer's first act was to switch it back to the twentieth century. Accordingly, I can promise you death.'

Her brain remained calm; her body steady, unaffected. No blood surged to her head. There was the barest quickening of her heartbeat. Her hands clenched with the tense knowledge that she must act faster, think faster. She thought : *If only Jack Garson were here, with his science, his swift, logical brain . . .*

Strangely then, she could feel her mind slipping out of her control, like sand between her fingers. Her body remained untroubled, untouched, but her mind was suddenly gliding down into dark depths. Terror came abruptly, as a score of flame streamers leaped into sight toward the ceiling. *Jack, Jack, help me! I need you! Oh, Jack, come –*

The slow seconds brought no answer; and the urgency of her need could brook no waiting. *Back home*, she thought. *I've got to get back home, back to the twentieth century.*

Her body twanged. There was blackness, and a horrible sensation of falling. The blow of the fall was not hard, and that unaffected, almost indestructible body of hers took the shock in a flash of pain-absorbing power. She grew aware of a floor with a rug on it. A dull light directly in front of her lost its distortion and became a window.

Her own apartment! She scrambled to her feet, and then poised motionless with dismay as the old, familiar, subtle vibration thrilled its intimate way along her nerves. The machine! The machine in the room below was working! Her will to safety had sent her back to her own time, but her call to Jack Garson had pressed unheard. And here she was, alone with only a strange, unwieldy power to help her against the gathering might of the enemy.

But that was her hope, that it was only gathering! Even Dr. Lell must have time to transport his forces. If she could get out of this building, use her power to carry her to safety, as it had already borne her from the time and space of the future. Carry her where? There was only one other place she could think of : To the hotel room from where she had launched herself with the key.

It wasn't death that came then, but a blow so hard that she was sobbing bitterly with the pain even as her mind yielded reluctantly to unconsciousness; even as she realized

55

in stark dismay that she had struck the wall of her apartment and this power she possessed had been betrayed once again by her inability to handle it. And now Dr Lell would have time to do everything necessary.

Blackness came.

CHAPTER TEN

There was a memory in Garson of the night, and the rushing machine that had carried him. It was a wonderful little metal thing that darted and twisted far to the left, as close to the red haze of the time-energy barrier as he dared to go. But not a machine had followed him. In seconds he was through the blazing gap, out of Delpa, safe from Dr. Lell.

Something had struck him then, a crushing blow ... He came out of sleep without pain, and with no sense of urgency. Drowsily, he lay, parading before his mind the things that had happened; and the comfortable realization came that he must be safe or he wouldn't be like this. There were things to do, of course. He must transmit the information to the Planetarians that they must conquer Delpa more swiftly, that final victory waited nowhere but in Delpa. And then, somehow, he must persuade them to let him return to Norma.

For a while he lay peacefully, his eyes open, gazing thoughtfully at a gay ceiling. From nearby, a man's voice said:

'There is no use expecting it.'

Garson turned his head, his first alert movement. A row of hospital-like cots stretched there, other rows beyond. From the nearest bed, a pair of fine, bright, cheerful eyes stared at him. The man lay with his head crotched in a bunched, badly rumpled pillow. He said:

'Expecting to feel surprised, I mean. You won't. You've been conditioned into recovering on a gradual scale, no excitement, no hysteria, nothing that will upset you. The doctors, though Planetarian trained, are all men of the past, and up to a day ago, they pronounced you —'

The man paused. His brown eyes darkened in a frown, then he smiled with an equally amazing grimness. 'I nearly said too much there. Actually, you may be strong enough, without getting yourself into a nervous state. Here's a preliminary warning: Toughen your mind for bad news.'

Garson had only the dimmest curiosity, and no sense of alarm at all. After what Dr. Lell had said directly and by implication of the Planetarians, no danger here could surpass what he had already been through. The only emotion he could sense within himself had to do with his double purpose of rescuing Norma from the recruiting station. He said aloud, 'If I should be asleep the next time a doctor or Planetarian comes in, will you waken me? I've got something to tell them.'

The man smiled mirthlessly. He was a personable looking young fellow around thirty. His reaction made Garson frown. His voice was sharp as he asked, 'What's the matter?'

The stranger shook his head half-pityingly. 'I've been twenty-seven days in this age,' he said, 'and I've never seen a Planetarian. As for telling anyone on the Planetarian side anything, I've already told you to expect bad news. I know you have a message to deliver. I even know from Dra Derrel what it is, but don't ask me how he found out. All I can say is, you'll have to forget about delivering any message to anyone. Incidentally, my name is Mairphy – Edard Mairphy.'

Garson was not interested in names or the mystery of how they knew his message. He was worried, however. Every word this gentle-faced, gentle-voiced young man had spoken was packed with tremendous implications. He stared at Mairphy, but there was only the frank, open face, the friendly, half-grim smile, the careless wisp of bright brown hair coming down over one temple – nothing at all of danger. Besides, where could any danger be coming from? From the Planetarians?

That was ridiculous. Regardless of their shortcomings, the Planetarians were the one race of this 'time' that must be supported. They might have curious, even difficult habits, but the other side was evil almost beyond imagination. Between them, there was no question of choice.

His course was simple. As soon as he was allowed to get up – and he felt perfectly well now – he would set out to make contact with a Planetarian. The whole affair was beginning to show unpleasant, puzzling aspects, but nothing serious. He grew aware of Mairphy's voice:

'The warning is all I'll say on that subject for the time being. There's something else, though. Do you think you'll be able to get up in an hour? I mean, do you feel all right?'

Garson nodded, puzzled. 'I think so. Why?'

'We'll be passing the moon about then, and I understand it's a sight worth seeing.'

'What?'

Mairphy stared at him contritely. He said slowly, 'I forgot. I was so busy not telling you about our main danger, it didn't occur to me that you were unconscious when we started.' He shrugged. 'Well, we're on our way to Venus; and even if there was nothing else, the cards would be stacked against you by that fact alone. There are no Planetarians aboard this ship, only human beings out of the past and tentacles of the Observer. There's not a chance in the world of you talking to any of them because –' He stopped, then, 'There, I nearly did it again. I'll let out the truth yet, before you ought to hear it.'

Garson paid scant attention. The shock wouldn't go away. He lay in a daze of wonder, overwhelmed by the incredible fact that he was in space. *In Space!* He felt outmaneuvered. Even the events he knew about would soon be a quarter of a million miles behind him.

The idea grew shocking. He sat rigidly, awkwardly, in the bed; and finally, in a choked voice, he said, 'How long will it take to get to Venus?'

'Ten days, I believe.'

Very cautiously, Garson allowed the figures to penetrate. Hope came again. It wasn't so bad as his first despairing thought had pictured it. Ten days to get there, ten days to persuade someone to let a Planetarian have a glimpse of his mind, ten days to get back to Earth. A month! He frowned. That wasn't so good. Wars had been lost, great empires collapsed in less time than that. Yet, how could he deliver his message on a Venus-bound spaceship? Courses of initial action suggested themselves, but one was clear.

He said in a troubled tone, 'If I were back where I came from, at this point I would try to see the captain of the ship. But you've made me doubt that normal procedures apply on a Planetarian spaceliner. Frankly, what are my chances?'

He saw that the young man was grim. 'Exactly none,' Mairphy replied. 'This is no joke, Garson. As I said before, Derrel knows and is interested in your message – don't ask me how or what or when. He was a political leader in his own age, and he's a marvel at mechanics, but, according to

59

him, he knows only the normal, everyday things of his life. You'll have to get used to the idea of being in with a bunch of men from past ages, some queer ducks among them, Derrel being the queerest of them all. But forget that. Just remember that you're on a spaceship in an age so far ahead of your own that there's not even a record of your time in the history books. Think hard about that!'

Garson thought, and he lay back, breathlessly still, dazzled once again by his strange environment, straining for impression. But there was no sense of movement, no abnormality at all. The world was quiet. The room seemed like an unusually large dormitory in a hospital. After a moment of tenseness, he allowed his body to relax, and the full, rich flood of thought to flow in. In that eager tide, the danger of which Mairphy had told him was like a figment of imagination, a shadow in remoteness. There was only the wonder, only Venus, and this silent, swift-plunging spaceship.

Venus! He let the word roll around in his mind, and it was exciting, intellectual fare, immensely stimulating to a mind shaped and trained as was his. Venus? For ages the dreams of men had reached into the skies, immeasurably fascinated by the mind staggering fact of other worlds as vast as their own; continents, seas, rivers, treasure beyond estimate. And now for him there was to be reality. Before that fact, other urgencies faded. Norma must be rescued, of course; the strange message delivered. But if it was to be his destiny to remain in this world until the end of the war, then he could ask nothing more of those years than this glowing sense of adventure, this shining opportunity to learn and see and know in a scientist's heaven.

He grew aware that Mairphy was speaking. 'You know' – the young man's voice was thoughtful – 'it's just possible that it might be a good idea if you did try to see the captain. I'll have to speak to Derrel before any further action is taken but –'

Garson sighed. He felt suddenly exhausted, mentally and physically, by the twisting course of events. 'Look,' he said wearily, 'a minute ago you stated it was absolutely impossible for me to see the captain; now it seems it might be a good idea and so the impossible becomes possible.'

A sound interrupted his words, a curious hissing sound that seemed to press at him. With a start he saw that men were climbing out of bed, groups that had been standing in quiet conversation were breaking up. In a minute, except for some three dozen who had not stirred from their beds, the manpower of that great room had emptied through a far door. As the door closed, Mairphy's tense voice stabbed at him:

'Quick! Help me out of bed and into my wheel chair. Damn this game leg of mine, but I've got to see Derrel. The attack must not take place until you've tried to see the captain. Quick, man!'

'Attack!' Garson began, then with an effort, caught himself. Forcing coolness through the shock that was gathering inside him, he lay back. He said in a voice that trembled, 'I'll help you up when you tell me what all this is about. Start talking. Fast!'

Mairphy sighed. 'The whole thing's really very simple. They herded together a bunch of skeptics – that's us; it means simply men who know they are in another age, and aren't superstitious about it, always potentially explosive, as the Planetarians well understood. But what they didn't realize was that Derrel was what he was. The mutiny was only partially successful. We got the control room, the engine room, but only one of the arsenals. The worst thing was that one of the tentacles escaped our trap, which means that the Observer Machine has been informed and that battleships have already been dispatched after us. Unless we gain full control fast, we'll be crushed; and the whole bunch of us will be executed out of hand.'

He continued, wih a bleak smile, 'That includes you and every person in this room, sick or innocent. The Planetarians leave the details of running their world in the hands of a monster machine called the Observer; and the Observer is mercilessly logical.' He shrugged, finished, 'That's what I meant by bad news. All of us are committed to victory or death. And now, quick! Help me get to Derrel and stop this attack!'

Garson's mind was a swollen, painful thing with the questions that quivered there: skeptics, tentacles, mutiny ... It was not until after Mairphy's power-driven wheel chair had vanished through the same door that had swallowed the men, that he realized how weary he was. He lay down on the bed, and there didn't seem to be a drop of emotion in him. He was thinking, a slow, flat, gray thought, of the part of

61

that message that had come to him in the depersonalizing machine, the solemn admonishment: *Take no unnecessary risks; stay alive!*

What a chance!

CHAPTER ELEVEN

The moon floated majestically against the backdrop of blank space, a great globe of light that grew and grew. He looked eagerly down at the side hidden from Earth and only vaguely photographed in his own day and age. Seen now, from space, he had a view of the relatively featureless surface. The Sea of Moscow and the great Soviet Mountains were still the most conspicuous objects, but in the central mass at this near distance, everything seemed rough and jagged, uneven.

For an hour the moon clung to size, but at last it began to retreat into distance. It was the gathering immensity of that distance that brought to Garson a sudden dark consciousness that he was again a tiny pawn in this gigantic struggle of gigantic forces.

He watched until the glowing sphere of moon was a shadowy pea-sized light half-hidden by the dominating ball of fire that was Earth. His immediate purpose was already a waxing shape in his mind, as he turned to stare down at Mairphy in his wheel chair. It struck him there were lines of fatigue around the other's eyes. He said, 'Now that the attack has been called off, I'd like to meet this mysterious Derrel. After which you'd better go straight to sleep.'

The younger man drooped. 'Help me to my bed, will you?'

From the bed, Mairphy smiled wanly. 'Apparently, I'm the invalid, not you. The paralyzer certainly did you no real harm, but the energy chopper made a pretty job of my right leg. By the way, I'll introduce you to Derrel when I wake up.'

Mairphy's slow, deep breathing came as a shock to Garson He felt deserted, at a loss for action, and finally annoyed at the way he had come to depend on the company of another man. For a while, he wandered around the room, half aimlessly, half in search of the extraordinary Derrel. But gradually his mind was drawn from that undetermined purpose. He became aware of the men from other times and places.

They swaggered, did these boys. When they stood, they leaned with casual grace, thumbs nonchalantly tucked into belts or into the armpits of strangely designed vests. Not more than half a dozen of that bold, vigorous-looking crew seemed to be the studious type. Here were men of the past, adventurers, soldiers of fortune, who had mutinied as easily as, under slightly different circumstances, they might have decided to fight for, instead of against, their captors.

Was it bad psychology on the part of the Planetarians? That seemed impossible because they were superbly skillful in the art. The explanation, of course, was that intelligence and ability as great as their own, or nearly as great, had entered the scene unknown to them, and easily duped the men of the past who operated the spaceship.

Derrel!

It brought a vivid awareness of the immense vitality of the life that had spawned over Earth through the ages. Here were men come full grown out of their own times, loving life, yet by their casual, desperate attempt at mutiny proving that they were not afraid of death.

One man was responsible, the activating force.

Three times Garson was sure that he had picked out Derrel, but each time he changed his mind before actually approaching the stranger. It was only gradually that he grew aware of a lank man. The first coherent picture he had was of a tall, somewhat awkward looking individual with a long face that was hollow-cheeked. The man was dressed in a gray shirt and gray trousers. Except for a look of cleanness about him, he could have stepped out of a farmhouse.

The man half stood, half leaned, in an ungraceful way against the side of one of the hospital-type beds, and he said nothing. Yet, somehow, he was the center of the group that surrounded him. The leader! After a moment Garson saw that the other was surreptitiously studying him. That was all he needed. He surveyed the man openly. Before his search-gaze, the deceptive, farmerish appearance of the other altered.

The hollow cheeks showed suddenly as a natural screen that distorted the almost abnormal strength of that face. The line of jaw ceased to be merely framework supporting the chin, showed instead in all its grim hardness, like the blunt edge of an anvil. The nose was strong and sharp, the face as a whole long and thin.

Garson's examination was interrupted. Somebody addressed the man as Mr. Derrel; and it was as if Derrel had been waiting for the words as for a signal. He stepped forward. He said in the calmest voice Garson had ever heard, 'Professor

64

Garson, do you mind if I speak to you' – he motioned forcefully yet vaguely – 'over there?'

Garson was amazed to find himself hesitating. For nearly an hour he had the purpose of finding this man, but now he realized he was reluctant to yield to the leadership of a stranger. It struck him sharply that even to agree to Derrel's simple request was to place himself, somehow, subtly under the man's domination.

Their eyes met, his own hard with thought, Derrel's at first expressionless, then smiling. The smile touched his face and lighted it in a most charming fashion. His entire countenance seemed to change. Briefly, the man's personality was so attractive that Garson's resistance seemed immature, even childish.

Garson was startled to hear himself say, 'Why, yes. What is it you wish?'

The answer was cool and of tremendous import. 'You have received a warning message, but you need look no further for its source. I am Dra Derrel of the Wizard race of Bor. My people are fighting under great difficulties to save a universe threatened by a war whose weapons are based on the time-energy cycle itself.'

'Just a minute!' Garson's voice was harsh in his own ears. 'Are you trying to tell me your people sent that message?'

'I am!' The man's face was almost gray-steel in color. 'And to explain that our position is now so dangerous that your own suggestion that you see Captain Larradin has become the most important necessity and the best plan.'

Strangely, it was that on which his mind fastened, not the revelation, but the mind picture of himself leaving the placid security of this room, delivering himself into the ruthless clutches of men from some other, more merciless past than his own – and to tentacles. Like a shadow overhanging every other emotion, he realized that the law of averages would not permit him to face death again without receiving it.

Slowly, the other thought – Derrel's revelation – began to intrude. He examined it, at first half puzzled that it continued to exist in his mind. Somehow, it wasn't really adequate, and certainly far from satisfactory as an explanation of all that had happened.

A message delivered into the black narrowness of a Glorious depersonalizing machine, hurtled across distance, through a web of Glorious defenses. From Derrel!

Garson frowned, his dissatisfaction growing. He stared at the man from slitted eyes; and saw that the other was standing in that peculiar easy-awkward posture of his, gazing at him coolly as if – the impression was a distinct one – as if waiting patiently for his considered reaction. That was reassuring, but it was far from being enough.

Garson said, 'I can see I've got to be frank, or this thing is going to be all wrong. My angle goes like this: I've been building a picture in my mind, an impossible picture I can see now, of beings with tremendous powers. I thought of them as possibly acting from the future of this future but, whatever their origin, I had confidence they were superhuman and super-Glorious.'

He stopped because the long-faced man was smiling in a twisted fashion. 'And now,' Derrel said wryly, 'the reality does not come up to your expectations. An ordinary man stands before you, and your dreams of god-power interfering in the affairs of men becomes what it always was basically: wishful thinking.'

'And in its place is what?' Garson questioned coolly.

Derrel took up the words steadily. 'In its place is a man who failed to take over a spaceship, and now faces death.'

Garson parted his lips to speak, then closed them again, puzzled. There was nothing so far but apparent honesty. Still, confession was far from being satisfactory explanation.

Derrel, his voice rich with the first hint of passion he had shown, said, 'I'm not sure it was such a great failure. I was one man manipulating strangers who had no reason to fight – many of them invalids – and yet I won a partial success against the highly trained crew of a completely mechanized space cruiser, a crew supported by no less than four tentacles of this omniscient Observer.'

Stripped as the account was, it brought a vivid flash of what the reality of that fight must have been. Flesh-and-blood men charging forward in the face of energy weapons, dealing and receiving desperate wounds, overwhelming the alert and adequate staff of an armored ship, and four tentacles, whatever they were. Tentacle – a potent, ugly word with inhuman implications.

And still the picture was not satisfactory. 'If you're going to use logic on this,' Garson said at last, slowly, 'you'll have to put up with my brand for another minute. Why did you

66

go in for mutiny in the first place under such difficult conditions?'

The man's eyes flashed with contemptuous fire. When he spoke, his voice was thick with emotion. 'Can you reasonably ask for more than the reality, which is that our position is desperate because we took risks? We took risks because' – he paused, as if gathering himself; then he continued tensely – 'because I am of the race of Wizards, and we were masters of the Earth of our time because we were bold. As was ever the way with Wizards, I chose the difficult, the dangerous path; and I tell you that victory, with all that it means, is not yet beyond our grasp.'

In the queerest fashion, the glowing voice died. An intent expression crept into the man's eyes. He tilted his head, as if listening for a remote sound. Garson shook the impression out of his mind, and returned to the thought that had been gatheriing while the other was speaking. He said coolly:

'Unfortunately, for all that emotion, I was trained to be a scientist, and I never learned to accept justification as a substitute for explanation.'

It was his turn to fall silent. With startled gaze he watched the tall, gawky figure stride at top speed along the wall. The Wizard man halted as swiftly as he started, but now his fingers were working with frantic speed at a section of the wall. As Garson came up, the wall slid free; and Derrel half-lowered, half-dropped it to the floor. In the hollow space revealed, wires gleamed; and a silver, shining glow-point showed. Unhesitatingly, Derrel rasped at the white-hot looking thing, and jerked. There was a faint flash of fire, and when his hand came away the glow was gone.

Derrel stared at Garson grimly. 'Those seeming wires are not wires at all, but a pure energy web, an electron mold that, over a period of about an hour, can mold a weapon where nothing existed before. Tentacles can focus that type of mold anywhere, and the mold itself is indestructible. But up to a certain stage the molded thing can be destroyed.'

Garson braced himself instinctively, as the other faced him squarely. Derrel said, 'You can see that without my special ability to sense energy formations, there would have been tragedy.'

67

'Without you,' Garson interjected, 'there would have been no mutiny. I'm sorry, but I've got the kind of mind that worries about explanations.'

Derrel gazed at him without hostility. He said finally, earnestly, 'I know your doubts, but you can see for yourself that I must go around examining our rather large territory for further electron-mold manifestations. Briefly, we Wizards are a race of the past who developed a science that enabled us to tap the time-ways of the Glorious, though we cannot yet build a time machine. In many ways, we are the superiors of both the Planetarians and the Glorious. Our mathematics showed us that the time-energy cycle could not stand strains beyond a certain point. Accordingly, we have taken, and are taking every possible action to save the universe, the first and most important necessity being that of establishing a base of operations, preferably a spaceship.' He finished quietly, 'For the rest, for the time being you must have faith. You must overcome your doubts, and go to see the captain. We must win this ship before we are overwhelmed. I leave you now to think it over.'

He whirled and strode off; and behind him he left partial conviction, mostly disbelief, but – Garson thought wryly – no facts. What a vague basis on which to risk the only life he had!

He found himself straining for sounds, but there was nothing except the idle conversation of the other men. The ship itself was quiet. It seemed to be suspended in this remote coign of the universe; and it at least was not restless. It flashed on in tireless, stupendous flight, but basically it was unhurried, isolated from mechanical necessities, knowing neither doubt nor hope, nor fear nor courage.

Doubt! His brain was an opaque mass flecked with the moving lights of thoughts, heavy with the gathering pall of his suspicion, knowing finally only one certainty: With so much at stake, he must find out more about the so-called Wizards of Bor. It would be foolish to make some move against the Planetarians, the hope of this war, on the glib say-so of anyone! But what to do? Where to find out?

The urgent minutes fled. There was the black, incredible vista of space. No answers offered there. There was lying in bed and staring at the gray ceiling; that was worse. Finally, there was the discovery of the library in a room adjoining the long dormitory; and that held such an immense promise that, for a brief hour, even the sense of urgency faded out of him.

Only gradually did he become aware that the books were a carefully selected collection. At any other time, every word of every page would have held him in thrall, but not now. For a while, with grim good humor, he examined volume after volume to verify his discovery. At last, weary with frustration, he returned to his bed. He found Mairphy awake.

His mind leaped; then he hesitated. It was possible he would have to approach the subject of Derrel warily. He said finally, 'I suppose you've been through the library.'

Mairphy shook his head, eyes slightly sardonic. 'Not that one. But on the basis of the two I have seen, I'll venture to guess they're elementary scientific books, travel books about planets, but no histories, and nowhere is there a reference to what year this is. They're not even letting us skeptics know that.'

Garson cut in almost harshly, 'These Planetarians are not such good angles as I thought. In an entirely different, perhaps cleverer way, this ship is organized to press us into their mold just as the Glorious used the deperson –'

He stopped, startled by the hard tenor of his thoughts. At this rate he'd soon work himself into an anti-Planetarian fury. Deliberately, he tightened his mind. His job was not to hate, but to ask careful questions about Derrel.

He parted his lips, but before he could speak, Mairphy said, 'Oh, the Planetarians are all right. If we hadn't gone in for this damned mutiny, we'd have been treated all right in the long run, provided we kept our mouths shut and conformed.'

Garson's mind wrenched itself from thought of Derrel. 'What do you mean?' he asked.

Mairphy laughed mirthlessly. 'We're the skeptics who, in a general way, know where we are. The great majority of recruits don't know anything except that it's a strange place. For psychological reasons, they've got to feel that they're in perfectly rational surroundings. Their own superstitions provide the solutions. An army of ancient Greeks think they're fighting on the side of Jupiter in the battle of the gods. Religious folk from about four hundred different ages think for reasons of their own that everything is as it should be. The Lerdite Moralists from the thirtieth century believe this is the war of the Great Machine to control its dissident elements.

69

And the Nelorian Dissenters of the year 7643 to 7699 – what's the matter?'

Garson couldn't help it. The shock was physical rather than mental. He hadn't, somehow, thought of it when Derrel talked of the Wizards of Bor, but now he was shaking. His nerves quivered from that casual, stunning array of words. He said finally, 'Don't mind me. It's those dates you've been handing out. I suppose it's really silly to think of time as being a past and a future. It's all these, spread out, six hundred billion Earths and universes created every minute.'

He drew a deep breath. Damn it, he'd stalled long enough. Any minute, Derrel would be coming back. He said stiffly, 'What about the Wizards of Bor? I heard somebody use the phrase, and it intrigued me.'

'Interesting race,' Mairphy commented, and Garson sighed with relief. The man suspected no ulterior motive. He waited tensely as Mairphy went on : 'The Wizards discovered some connection between sex and the mind which gave them superintellect, including mental telepathy. Ruled the Earth for about three hundred years, just before the age of Endless Peace set in. Power politics and all that, violence, great on mechanics, built the first true spaceship which, according to description, was as good as any that has ever existed since. Most of their secrets were lost. Those that weren't became the property of a special priest clique whose final destruction is a long story.'

He paused, frowning thoughtfully, while Garson wondered bleakly how he ought to be taking all this. So far, Derrel's story was substantiated practically word for word. Mairphy's voice cut into his indecision. 'There's a pretty story about how the spaceship was invented. In their final struggle for power, a defeated leader, mad with anxiety about his beautiful wife who had been taken as a mistress by the conqueror, disappeared, returned with the ship, got his wife and his power back; and the Derrel dynasty ruled for a hundred years after that.'

'Derrel!' Garson said. 'The Derrel dynasty!'

The echo of the shock yielded to time and familiarity, and died. They talked about it in low tones; and their hushed baritones formed a queer, deep-throated background to the measured beat of Garson's thoughts.

He stepped back, finally, as Mairphy eagerly called other men. With bleak detachment, he listened while Mairphy's voice recast itself over and over into the same shape, the same story, though the words and even the tone varied with each telling. Always, however, the reaction of the men was the same – joy! Joy at the certainty of victory! And what did it matter what age they went to afterwards?

Garson grew abruptly aware that Mairphy was staring at him sharply. Mairphy said, 'What's the matter?'

He felt the weight of other eyes on him as he shrugged and said, 'All this offers little hope for me. History records that we won this ship. But I have still to confront the captain, and history is silent as to whether I lived or died. Frankly, I consider the message that I received in the Glorious depersonalizing machine more important than ever, and accordingly my life's of more importance than that of anyone else on this ship. I repeat, our only certainty is that Derrel escaped with the spaceship. But who else lived, we don't know. Derrel –'

'Yes?' said the calm voice of Derrel behind him. 'Yes, Professor Garson?'

Garson turned slowly. He had no fixed plan; there was the vaguest intention to undermine Derrel's position, and that made him stress the uncertainty of any of the men escaping. But it wasn't a plan, because there was the unalterable fact that the ship had gotten away. Derrel had won.

No plan. The only factors in his situation were his own tremendous necessities and the inimical environment in which they existed. For a long moment, he stared at the gangling body, studied the faint triumph that gleamed in the abnormally long yet distinctive face of the Wizard man. Garson said, 'You can read minds. So it's unnecessary to tell you what's going on. What are your intentions?'

Derrel smiled, the glowing, magnetic smile that Garson had already seen. His agate eyes shone as he surveyed the circle of men; then he began to speak in a strong, resonant voice. There was command in that voice, and a rich, powerful personality behind it, the voice of a man who had won.

'My first intention is to tell everyone here that we are going to an age that is a treasure house of spoils for bold men. Women, palaces, wealth, power for every man who follows me to the death. You know yourself what a damned barren world we're in now. No women, never anything for us but the prospect of facing death fighting the Glorious still entrenched on Venus or Earth. And a damned bunch of moral-

71

ists fighting a war to the finish over some queer idea that men ought or ought not have birth control. Are you with me?'

It was a stirring, a ringing appeal to basic impulses, and the answer could not have been more satisfactory. A roar of voices, cheers; and finally, 'What are we waiting for? Let's get going!'

The faint triumph deepened on Derrel's face as he turned back to Garson. He said softly, 'I'm sorry I lied to you, Professor, but it never occured to me that Mairphy or anybody aboard would know my history. I told you what I did because I had read in your mind some of the purposes that moved your actions. Naturally, I applied the first law of persuasion, and encouraged your hopes and desires.'

Garson smiled grimly. The little speech Derrel had just given to the men was a supreme example of the encouragement of hopes and desires, obviously opportunistic, insincere and reliable only if it served the other's future purposes.

He saw that Derrel was staring at him, and he said, 'You know what's in my mind. Perhaps you can give me some of that easy encouragement you dispense. But remember, it's got to be based on logic. That includes convincing me that, if I go to the captain, it is to your self-interest to set me down near a Planetarian stronghold, and that furthermore –'

The words, all the air in his lungs, hissed out of his body. There was a hideous sense of pressure. He was jerked off his feet, and he had the flashing, uncomprehending vision of two beds passing by beneath him. Then he was falling.

Instinctively, he put out his hand, and took the desperate blow of the crash onto a third bed. He sprawled there, stunned, dismayed, but unhurt and safe.

Safe from what? He clawed himself erect, and stood swaying, watching other men pick themselves up, becoming aware for the first time of groans and cries of pain. A voice exploded into the room from some unseen source:

'Control room speaking! Derrel – the damnedest thing has happened. A minute ago, we were thirty million miles from Venus. Now, the planet's just ahead, less then two million miles, plainly visible. What's happened?'

Garson saw Derrel then. The man was lying on his back on the floor, his eyes open, an intent expression on his face. The Wizard man waved aside his extended hands.

'Wait!' Derrel said sharply. 'The tentacle aboard this ship has just reported to the Observer on Venus, and is receiving a reply, an explanation of what happened. I'm trying to get it.'

His voice changed, became a monotone. 'The seventeenth X space and time manipulations ... taking place somewhere in the future ... several years from now. Your spaceship either by accident or design caught in the eddying current in the resulting time storm. Still no clue to the origin of the mighty powers being exercised. That is all ... except that battleships are on the way from Venus to help you.'

Derrel stood up; he said quietly, 'About what you were saying, Garson, there is no method by which I can prove that I will do anything for you. History records that I lived out my full span of life. Therefore, no self-interest, no danger to the universe, can affect my existence in the past. You'll have to act on the chance that the opportunity offers for us to give you assistance later, and there's no other guarantee I can give.'

That was at least straightforward. Of course, to an opportunist, even truth was but a means to an end, a means of lulling suspicion. There remained the hard fact that *he* must take the risks. He said, 'Give me five minutes to think it over. You believe, I can see, that I will go.'

Derrel nodded. 'Your mind is beginning to accept the idea.'

There was no premonition in Garson of the fantastic thing that was going to happen. He thought, a gray, cold thought: So he was going! In five minutes.

CHAPTER TWELVE

He stood finally at the wall visiplate, staring out at the burnished immensity of Venus. The planet, already vast, was expanding visibly, like a balloon being blown up. Only it didn't stop expanding, and, unlike an overgrown balloon, it didn't burst.

The tight silence was broken by the tallest of the three handsome Ganellians. The man's words echoed, not Garson's thoughts, but the tenor, the dark mood of them. 'So much beauty proves once again that war is the most completely futile act of this 'future,' there are people who know who won this war; and they're doing nothing – damn them!'

Garson's impulse was to say something, to add once more his own few facts to that fascinating subject. But instead he held his thought hard on the reality of what he must do in a minute.

Besides, Mairphy had described the Ganellians as emotional weaklings who had concentrated on beauty, and with whom it was useless to discuss anything. It was true, of course, that he himself had given quite a few passable displays of emotionalism.

The thought ended as Mairphy said impatiently, 'We've discussed all that before, and we're agreed that either the people of the future do not exist at all – which means the universe was blown up in due course by the Glorious energy barrier – or, if the people of the future exist, they're simply older versions of the million-year-old bodies of the Planetarians or Glorious. If they exist, then the universe was not destroyed, so why should they interfere in the war?

'Finally, we're agreed that it's impossible that the people of the future, whatever their form, are responsible for the message that came through to Professor Garson. If they can get through a message at all, why pick Garson? Why not contact the Planetarians direct? Or even warn the Glorious of the danger!'

Garson said, 'Derrel, what is your plan of attack?'

The reply was cool. 'I'm not going to tell you that. Reason: at close range a tentacle can read any unwary mind. I want you to concentrate on the thought that your purpose is aboveboard; don't even think of an attack in connection with it. Wait – don't reply! I'm going to speak to Captain Larradin!'

'What . . .' Garson began, and stopped.

The Wizard man's eyes were closed, his body rigid. He said, half to Garson, half to the others, 'A lot of this stuff here works by mind control.' His voice changed. 'Captain Larradin!'

There was a tense silence; then a hard voice literally spat into the room, 'Yes!'

Derrel said, 'We have an important communication to make. Professor Garson, one of the men who was unconscious when –'

'I know the one you mean,' interrupted that curt voice. 'Get on with your communication.'

Derrel said, 'Professor Garson has just become conscious and he has the answer to the phenomena that carried this spaceship thirty million miles in thirty seconds. He feels that he must see you immediately and communicate his message to the Planetarians at once.'

There was a burst of cold laughter. 'What fools we'd be to let any of you come here until after the battleships arrive! And that's my answer: He'll have to wait till the battleships arrive.'

'His message,' said Derrel, 'cannot wait. He's coming down now, alone.'

'He will be shot on sight.'

'I can well imagine,' Derrel said scathingly, 'what the Planetarians will do to you if he is shot. This has nothing to do with the rest of us. He's coming because he must deliver that message. That is all.'

Before Garson could speak, Mairphy said in a distinct voice, 'I'm opposed to it. I admit I accepted the plan earlier, but I couldn't favor it under such circumstances.'

The Wizard man whirled on him. His voice was a vibrant force as he raged, 'That was a stab in the back to all of us. Here is a man trying to make up his mind on a dangerous mission, and you project a weakening thought. You have said that you come from the stormy period following the thirteen thousand years of Endless Peace. That was after my time, and I know nothing about the age, but it is evident that the softness of the peace period still corroded your people. As a cripple, a weakling who is not going to do any of the fighting, you will kindly refrain from giving further advice!'

It could have been devastating, but Mairphy simply shrugged, smiled gently, unaffectedly at Garson, and said, 'I withdraw from the conversation.' He finished, 'Good luck, friend!'

Derrel, steely-eyed and cold-voiced, said to Garson, 'I want to point out one thing. History says we conquered this ship. The only plan we have left revolves around you. Therefore, you went to see the captain.'

To Garson, to whom logic was the great prime mover, that thought had already come. Besides, his mind had been made up for five minutes.

The second corridor was empty too, and that strained Garson's tightening nerves to the breaking point. He paused stiffly, and wiped the thin line of perspiration from his brow. And still he had no premonition of the incredible ending that was coming. There was nothing but the deadly actuality of his penetration into the depths of a ship that seemed of endless length, and seemed larger with each step that he took.

A door yielded to his touch. He peered into a great storeroom, piled with freight, thousands of tons, silent and lifeless as the corridors ahead. He walked on, his mind blanker now, held steadily away from the thought of Derrel's intended attack. He thought vaguely : *If Norma could keep from Dr. Lell her action of writing a letter to me, then I can keep my thoughts from anyone or anything.*

He was so intent that he didn't see the side corridor until the men burst from it, and they had him before he could think of fighting. Not that he intended to fight.

'Bring him in here!' said a hard, familiar voice; and after a moment of peering into the shadows of the receding corridor, he saw a slender man in uniform standing beside a tentacle!

The hard, young-sounding voice said, 'To hell with the Observer. We can always execute. Bring him in here!'

A door opened, and light splashed out. The door closed behind him. Garson saw that the room was no more than a small anteroom to some vaster, darkened room beyond. He scarcely noticed that. He was thinking with a stinging shock of fury : *The logical Observer advising execution without a hearing. Why, that isn't reasonable. Damn the stupid Observer!*

His fury faded into vast surprise as he stared at the captain. His first impression had been that the other was a young man, but at this closer view he looked years older, immeasurably more mature. And somehow, in his keyed-up state, the observation astonished him. His amazement ended as his mind registered the blazing question in Captain Larradin's eyes. Quickly, Garson launched into his story.

When he had finished, the commander turned his hard face to the tentacle, 'Well?' he said.

The tentacle's voice came instantly, coldly. 'The Observer recalls to your memory its earlier analysis of this entire situation: The destruction of Tentacles 1601, 2 and 3 and the neutralization of electron molds could only have been accomplished with the assistance of a mind reader. Accordingly, unknown to us, a mind reader is aboard. Four races in history solved the secret of the training essential to mental telepathy. Of these, only the Wizards of Bor possessed surpassing mechanical ability –'

It was the eeriness that held his whole mind at first, the fantastic reality of this *thing* talking and reasoning like a human being. The Observer Machine of the Glorious that he had seen was simply a large machine, too big to grasp mentally; like some gigantic number, it was there, and that was all. But this long tubular monstrosity with its human voice was alien.

The eerie feeling ended in hard, dismaying realization that a creature that could analyze Derrel's identity might actually prove that death was his own logical lot, and that all else was illusion. The dispassionate voice went on:

'Wizard men are bold, cunning and remorseless, and they take no action in an emergency that is not related to their purpose. Therefore, this man's appearance is part of a plot. Destroy him and withdraw from the ship. The battleship will take all necessary action later, without further loss of life.'

Garson saw, with a sudden, desperate fear, that Captain Larradin was hesitating. The commander said unhappily, 'Damn it, I hate to admit defeat.'

'Don't be tedious!' said the tentacle. 'Your forces *might* win, but the battleship *will* win.'

Decision came abruptly. 'Very well,' said the captain curtly. 'Willant, de-energize this prisoner and –'

Garson said in a voice that he scarcely recognized, an abnormally steady voice, 'What about my story?'

77

There was a moment of silence.

'Your story,' the tentacle said finally – and Garson's mind jumped at the realization that it was the tentacle, and not the captain, who answered – 'your story is rejected by the Observer as illogical. It is impossible that anything went wrong with a Glorious depersonalizing machine. The fact that you were repersonalized after the usual manner on reaching our lines is evidence of your condition, because the repersonalizing machine reported nothing unusual in your case.

'Furthermore, even if it was true, the message you received was stupid, because no known power or military knowledge could force the surrender of Delpa one minute sooner. It is impossible to neutralize a time-energy barrier except in the way that it is being done; any other method would destroy the neutralizing machine. The military maneuver being used is the ultimate development of dimensional warfare in a given area of space. And so –'

The words scarcely penetrated, though all the sense strained through, somehow. His mind was like an enormous weight, dragging at one thought, one hope. He said, fighting for calmness now, 'Commander, by your manner to this tentacle and its master, I can see that you have long ago ceased to follow its conclusions literally. Why? Because it's inhuman. The Observer is a great reservoir of facts that can be co-ordinated on any subject, *but it is limited by the facts it knows*. It's a machine, and, while it may be logical to destroy me before you leave the ship, you know and I know that it is neither necessary nor just, and what is overwhelmingly more important, it can do no harm to hold me prisoner, and make arrangements for a Planetarian to examine the origin of the message that came to me.'

He finished in a quiet, confident tone, 'Captain, from what one of the men told me, you're from the 2000s A.D. I'll wager they still had horse races in your day. I'll wager, furthermore, that no machine could ever understand a man getting a hunch and betting his bottom dollar on a dark horse. You've already been illogical in not shooting me at sight, as you threatened on the communicator; in not leaving the ship as the Observer advised; in letting me talk here even as the attack on your enemies is beginning – for there is an attack of some kind, and it's got the best brain on this ship behind it. But that's unimportant because you're going to abandon

78

ship. What is important is this: You must carry your illogic to its logical conclusion. Retrieve your prestige, depend for once in this barren life here on luck and luck alone.'

The hard eyes did not weaken by a single gleam, but the hard voice spoke words that sounded like purest music. 'Willant, take this prisoner into the lifeboat.'

It was at that moment it happened. With victory in his hands, the knowledge that more than two years remained before the time energy barrier would be threatening the universe, the whole, rich, tremendous joy that he had won everything – all of that, and unutterable relief, and more, was in his brain when –

A voice came into his mind, strong and clear and as irresistible as living fire, a woman's voice. Norma's!

Jack, Jack, help me! I need you! Oh, Jack, come –

The universe spun. Abruptly, there was no ship, and he was pitching into a gulf of blackness. Inconceivable distance fell behind him.

There was no ship, no earth, no light.

Time must have passed, for slow thought was in him; and the night remained. No not night. He could realize that now, for there was time to realize. It was not night, it was emptiness. Nothingness!

Briefly, the scientist part of his brain grasped at the idea; the possibility of exploring, of examining this nonspace. But there was nothing to examine, nothing in him to examine *with*, no senses that could record or comprehend – nothingness! He felt dismay then, a black wave of it. His brain shrank from the terrible strain of impression. But, somehow, time passed. The flood of despair streamed out of him. There remained only nothingness!

Change came abruptly. One instant there was that complete isolation. The next, a man's voice said matter of factly, 'This one is a problem. How the devil did he get into the configuration of the upper arc? You'd think he fell in.'

'No report of any planes passing over Delpa,' said a second voice. 'Better ask the Observer if there's any way of getting him out.'

Figuratively, gravely, his mind nodded in agreement to that. He'd have to get out, of course.

His brain paused. Out of where? Nothingness?

For a long tense moment, his thought poised over that

tremendous question, striving to penetrate the obscure depths of it that seemed to waver just beyond the reach of his reason. There had been familiar words spoken.

Delpa! An ugly thrill chased through his mind. He wasn't in Delpa – he felt abruptly, horribly sick – or was he?

The sickness faded into a hopeless weariness, almost a chaotic dissolution. What did it matter where he was? Once more, he was a complete prisoner of a powerful, dominating environment, prey to forces beyond his control, unable to help Norma, unable to help himself.

Norma! He frowned mentally, empty of any emotion, unresponsive even to the thought that what had happened implied some enormous and deadly danger for Norma. There was only the curious, almost incredible way that she had called him; and nightmarishly he had fallen – toward Delpa! Fallen into an insane region called the configuration of the upper arc. With a start, he realized that the Observer's voice had been speaking for some seconds:

'. . . it can be finally stated that no plane, no machine of any kind, has flown over Delpa since the seventeenth time and space manipulation four weeks ago. Therefore, the man you have discovered in the upper arc is an enigma whose identity must be solved without delay. Call your commander.'

He waited, for there was nothing to think about, at least not at first. He recalled finally that the spaceship had been pulled a million miles a second by the mysterious seventeenth manipulation of time and space; only Derrel had distinctly described it as a repercussion from several years in the future. Now, the Observer talked as if it had happened four weeks ago. Funny!

'Nothing funny about it!' said a fourth voice, a voice so finely pitched, so directed into the stream of his thought that he wondered briefly, blankly, whether he had thought the words, or spoken them himself; then, 'Professor Garson, you are identified. The voice you are hearing is that of a Planetarian who can read your mind.'

A *Planetarian!* Relief made a chaos of his brain. With an effort, he tried to speak, but he seemed to have no tongue, or lips, or body. He had nothing but his mind there in that emptiness; his mind revolving swiftly, ever more swiftly around the host of things he simply had to know. It was the voice, the cool, sane voice, and the stupendous things it was saying, that gradually quieted the turmoil that racked him.

'The answer to what worries you most is that Miss Matheson was the center of the seventeenth space and time manipulation, the first time a human being has been used.

'The manipulation consisted of withdrawing one unit of the Solar System from the main stream without affecting the continuity of the main system; one out of the ten billion a second was swung clear in such a fashion that the time-energy cycle with its senseless, limitless power began to re-create it, carrying on two with the same superlative ease as formerly with only one.

'Actually, there are now eighteen solar systems existing roughly parallel to each other – seventeen manipulated creations and the original. My body, however, exists in only two of these because none of the previous sixteen manipulations occurred in my lifetime. Naturally, these two bodies of mine exist in separate worlds and will never again have contact with each other.

'Because she was the center of activity, Norma Matheson has her being in the main solar system only. The reason your physical elements responded to her call is that she now possesses the Insel mind power. Her call merely drew you toward her, not to her, because she lacks both the intelligence and the knowledge necessary for the competent employment of her power.

'As Miss Matheson did not protect you from intermediate dangers, you fell straight into the local time-energy barrier surrounding the city of Delpa, which promptly precipitated you into the time emptiness where you now exist. Because of the angle of your fall, it will require an indefinite period for the machines to solve the equation that will release you. Until then, have patience.'

'Wait!' Garson said urgently. 'The great time-energy barrier! It should be completed about now!'

'In two weeks at most,' came the cool reply. 'We received your story, all right, and transmitted the startling extent of the danger to the Glorious. In their pride and awful determination, they see it merely as a threat to make us surrender – or else! To us, however, the rigidly controlled world they envision means another form of death – a worse form. No blackmail will make us yield, and we have the knowledge that people of the future sent the warning. Therefore, we won!'

There was no time to think that over carefully. Garson phrased his next question hurriedly. 'Suppose they're not of the future, not of this seventeenth, or is it eighteenth, solar system? What will happen to me if this solar system explodes out of existence?'

The answer was cooler still. 'Your position is as unique as that of Miss Matheson. You fell out of the past into the future; you missed the manipulation. Therefore you exist, not in two solar systems, but only where you are, attached in a general way to us. Miss Matheson exists only in the main system. There is no way to my knowledge that you two can ever come together again. Accustom yourself to that idea.'

That was all. His next question remained unanswered. Time passed and his restless spirit drooped. Life grew dim within him. He lay without thought on the great, black deep. Immense, immeasurable time passed, and he waited, but no voices came to disturb his cosmic grave. Twice, forces tugged at him. The first time, he thought painfully: The time-energy barrier of the Glorious had been completed, and the pressure, the tugging, was all he felt of the resulting destruction.

If that had happened, nothing, no one, would ever come to save him!

That first tugging, and the thought that went with it, faded into remoteness, succumbed to the weight of the centuries, was lost in the trackless waste of the aeons that slid by. And finally, when it was completely forgotten, when every plan of action, every theory, every hope and despair had been explored to the nth degree – the second tug of pressure came.

A probing sensation it was, as if he was being examined; and finally a flaming, devastatingly powerful thought came at him from outside!

I judge it an extrusion from a previous universe, a very low form of life, intelligence .007, unworthy of our attention. It must be registered for its infinitesimal influence and interference with energy flowage – and cast adrift.

CHAPTER THIRTEEN

Returning consciousness stirred in Norma's body. She felt the sigh that breathed from her lips. Dimly, she grew aware that she must leave this place. But there was not yet enough life in her nerves, no quickening of the co-ordination, the concentration, so necessary to the strange, masochistic power she had been given. She thought drearily : *If only I had gone to a window instead of projecting myself against an impenetrable wall.* She must get to the breakfast-nook window that overlooked the roof.

She stood at the window instantly, weary with pain, startled by the swift reaction to her thought. Hope came violently. She thought; *Pain – no pain can touch me.*

Behind her, footsteps and other, strange sounds crashed on the stairway; behind her, the outer door blinked into ravenous flame. Ahead was the dark, lonely night. She scrambled to the sill. In her ears was the sound of the things that were swarming into her apartment. Then she was at the edge of the roof, and she could see the milling beast men on the sidewalk below, and she could see the street corner a hundred yards away.

Instantly, she was at the corner, standing lightly, painlessly, on the pavement. But there were too many cars for further 'power' travel, cars that would make devastatingly hard walls.

As she paused in a desperate uncertainty, one of the cars slowed to a stop; and it was the simplest thing to run forward, open the door and climb in, just as it started up again. There was a small man crouching in dimness behind the steering wheel. To him, she said, almost matter-of-factly, 'Those men! They're chasing me!'

A swarm of the beast men wallowed awkwardly into the revealing glow of the corner light, squat, apelike, frightening things. The driver yelped shrilly, 'Good God!' The car accelerated.

The man began to babble, 'Get out! Get out! I can't afford to get mixed up in a thing like this. I've got a family – wife – children – waiting for me this instant at home. Get out!'

He shoved at her with one hand, as if he would somehow

push her through the closed door. And, because her brain was utterly pliant, utterly geared to flight, she had no real resistance. A neon light a block away caught her gaze, and she said, 'See that taxi stand? Let me off there.'

By the time she climbed out, tentacles were glittering shapes in the air above the dim street behind her. She struck at them with her mind, but they only sagged back, like recoiling snakes, still under control, obviously prepared now for her power.

In the taxi, her mind reverted briefly in astounded thought: That mouse of a man! Had she actually let him control her, instead of forcing the little pipsqueak to her mighty will –

Will! She must use her will. No tentacle can come within – within – She'd have to be practical. How far had they retreated from her power? Half a mile? No tentacle can come within half a mile of this car. Eagerly, she stared out of the rear window, and her eyes widened as she saw they were a hundred yards away and coming closer. *What was wrong?* In shrinking expectation she waited for the devastating fire of third-order energies, and when it did not come, she thought: *This car must be made to go faster!*

There were other cars ahead, and some passing, but altogether not many. There was room for terrible speed if she had the courage, didn't lose control, and if the power would work. *Through there,* she directed, *and through there and around that corner* –

She heard yells from the driver, but for a time the very extent of his dismay brought encouragement. That faded bleakly as the tentacles continued their glittering course behind her, sometimes close, sometimes far away, but always relentlessly on her trail, unshakably astute in frustrating every twist of her thought, every turn of the car, every hope.

But why didn't they attack? There was no answer to that as the long night of flight dragged on, minute by slow minute. Finally, pity touched her for the almost mad driver, who half-sat, half-swooned behind the steering wheel, held to consciousness and to sanity – she could see in his mind – only by the desperate knowledge that this car was his sole means of livelihood and nothing else mattered besides that, not even death.

Let him go, she thought. It was sheer cruelty to include him in the fate that was gathering out of the night for her.

84

Let him go, but not yet. At first, she couldn't have told what the purpose was that quivered in her mind. But it was there, deep and chill and like death itself, and she kept directing the car without knowing exactly where she was going.

Conscious understanding of her unconscious will to death came finally, as she climbed to the ground and saw the glint of river through the trees of a park. And knew her destiny. Here in this park, beside this river, where nearly four years before she had come starving and hopeless to commit suicide – here she would make her last stand!

She watched the tentacles floating toward her through the trees, catching little flashing glimpses of them as the dim electric lights of the park shimmered against their metallic bodies; and she felt a vast wonder, untainted by fear. Was this real? Was it possible that there was no one, no weapon, no combination of air, land and sea forces, nothing that could protect her?

In sudden exasperation, she thrust her power at the nearest glint. And laughed a curt, futile laugh when the thing did not even quiver. So far as the tentacles were concerned, her power had been nullified. The implications were ultimate. When Dr. Lell arrived, he would bring swift death to her.

She scrambled down the steep bank to the dark edge of the sullen river; and the intellectual mood that had brought her here to this park, where once she had wanted death, filled her being. She stood taut, striving for a return of the emotion, for the thought of it was not enough. If only she could recapture the black, emotional mood of that other dark night!

A cool, damp breeze whisked her cheeks; but she could not muster the desire to taste those ugly waters. She wanted, not death, nor power, nor the devastation of third-order energies, but marriage, a home with green grass and a flower garden. She wanted life, contentment – Garson!

It was more of a prayer than a command that rose from her lips in that second call for help, an appeal from the depths of her need to the only man who in all these long, deadly years had been in her thoughts: *Jack, wherever you are, come to me here on Earth, come through the emptiness of time, come safely without pain, without bodily hurt or damage, and with mind clear. Come now!*

With a dreadful start, she jerked back. For a man stood beside her there by the dark waters!

The breeze came stronger. It brought a richer, more tangy smell of river stingingly into her nostrils. But it wasn't physical revival she needed. It was her mind again that was slow to move, her mind that had never yet reacted favorably to her power, her mind lying now like a cold weight inside her. The figure stood with stonelike stolidity, like a lump of dark, roughly shaped clay given a gruesome half-life. She thought in ghastly dismay: Had she recalled from the dead into dreadful existence a body that may have been lying in its grave for generations?

The thing stirred and became a man. Garson said in a voice that sounded hesitant and huskily unnatural in his own ears, 'I've come – but my mind is only clearing now. And speech is hard after a quadrillion years.' He shuddered with the thought of the countless ages he had spent in eternity; then, 'I don't know what happened. I don't know what danger made you call me a second time, or whether any exists; but whatever the situation, I've thought it all out.

'You and I are being used by the mysterious universe manipulators because, according to their history, we *were* used. They would not have allowed us to get into such desperate straits if they could come to us physically, and yet it is obvious that everything will fail for them, for us, unless they can make some direct physical contact and show us how to use the vast power you have been endowed with. They must be able to come only through some outside force, and only yours exists in our lives. Therefore, call them, call them in any words, for they must need only the slightest assistance. Call them, and afterward we can talk and plan and hope.'

She began to have thoughts then, and questions – all the questions that had ever puzzled her. Why had Dr. Lell kept repeating that she had made no trouble according to the Glorious historical record of her, when trouble was all she had ever given? Why had she been able to defeat the first tentacle, and yet now her power, that had called Jack Garson from some remote time, was futile against them? And where was Dr. Lell? With an effort she finally roused her brain from its repetitious pondering over paradoxes. What words she used then, she could not have repeated, for she remembered nothing of them a moment after they were spoken. In her mind was only a fascinated horror of expectation that grew and grew as a sound came from the water near her feet.

The water stirred. It sighed as if yielding to some body

that pressed its dark elements. It gurgled in a way that gave her a feeling of queer, obscene horror, and a body blacker than itself, and bigger than any man, made a glinting, ugly rim of foam.

It was Jack Garson's fingers, strong and unflinching, grasping her, and his hard, determined voice that prevented her from uttering the panicky words of demon exorcise that quivered at the edge of her mind.

'Wait!' he said. 'It's victory, not defeat. Wait!'

'Thank you, Professor Garson!' The voice that came out of the darkness held a strange, inhuman quality that kept her taut and uneasy. It went on, 'For your sakes, I could approach in no other way. We of the four hundred and ninetieth century A.D. are human in name only. There is a dreadful irony in the thought that war, the destroyer of men, finally changed man into a beastlike creature. One solace remains: We saved our minds at the expense of our bodies.

'Your analysis was right, Professor Garson, as far as it went. The reason we cannot use a time machine from our age is that our whole period will be in a state of abnormal unbalance for hundreds of thousands of years; even the tiniest misuse of energy could cause unforseeable changes in the fabric of the time-energy cycle, which is so utterly indifferent to the fate of men. Our method could only be the indirect and partially successful one of isolating the explosion on one of eighteen solar systems, and drawing all the others together to withstand the shock. This was not so difficult as it sounds, for time yields easily to simple pressures.

'Miss Matheson, the reason the tentacles could trail you is that you were being subjected to psychological terrors. The tentacles that have been following you through the night were not real, but third-order light projections of tentacles, designed to keep you occupied till Dr. Lell could bring his destroyer machines to bear. Actually, you have escaped all their designs. How? I have said time yields to proper pressures. Such a pressure existed as you stood by the river's edge trying to recall the mood of suicide. It was easier for you to have power to slip through time to that period nearly four years earlier than for you to recapture an unwanted lust for self-inflicted death.'

'Good heavens!' Garson gasped. 'Are you trying to tell us that this is that night, and that a few minutes from now Dr. Lell will come along and hire a desperate girl sitting on a park bench to be a front for a fake Calonian recruiting station?

'And this time,' said the inhuman voice, 'the history of the Glorious will be fulfilled. She will make no trouble.'

Garson had the sudden desperate sensation of being beyond his depth. 'What – what about our bodies that existed then? I thought two bodies of the same person couldn't exist in the same time and space.'

'They can't!'

'But –'

The firm, alien voice cut him off, cut off, too, Norma's sudden, startled intention to speak. 'There are no paradoxes in time. I have said that, in order to resist the destruction of the isolated eighteenth solar system, the other seventeen were brought together into one – this one! The only one that now exists! But the others *were*, and in some form you were in them. But now you are here, and this is the real and only world.

'I leave you to think that over, for now you must act. History says that you two took out a marriage license – tomorrow. History says Norma Garson had no difficulty leading the double life of wife of Professor Garson and slave to Dr. Lell; and that, under my direction, she learned to use her power until the day came to destroy the great energy barrier of Delpa and help the Planetarians to their rightful victory.'

Garson was himself again. 'Rightful?' he said. 'I'm not so convinced of that. They were the ones who precipitated the war by breaking the agreement for population curtailment.'

'Rightful,' said the voice firmly, 'because they first denounced the agreement on the grounds that it would atrophy the human spirit and mind. They fought the war on a noble plane, and offered compromise until the last moment. No automatons are on their side, and all the men they directly recruited from the past were plainly told they were wanted for dangerous work. Most of them were unemployed veterans of past wars.'

Norma found her voice, 'That second recruiting station I saw, with the Greeks and the Romans –'

'Exactly. But now you must receive your first lesson in the intricate process of mind and thought control, enough to fool Dr. Lell –'

The odd part of it was that, in spite of all the words that

88

had been spoken, the warm glow of genuine belief didn't come to her until she sat in the dim light on the bench, and watched the gaunt body of Dr. Lell stalking out of the shadowed path. Poor, unsuspecting superman!

The
Three Eyes of Evil

CHAPTER ONE

BEFORE THE CORONER'S JURY
STATEMENT OF THOMAS BARRON

My name is Thomas Barron. For nine years I have been a partner in the brokerage firm of Slade & Barron. I never suspected Michael Slade was abnormal. He was a strong character, and I always thought him rather a superior individual.

I saw him a dozen times after the car accident that precipitated events, mostly in connection with my purchase of his share of the business. He gave me no inkling of anything wrong, and I have no idea what actually happened.

The crash was over, the car neatly turned on its top. Slade sprawled dizzily on his back, conscious that he had lost his glasses. Something warm trickled from his forehead into his left eye.

He wiped it away, and saw with a start that it was blood. He mustered a smile for his wife, who was sitting up. He said:

'Well, we survived. I don't know what happened. The steering gear broke, I think.'

He stopped. Miriam was close enough for his nearsighted eyes, even without glasses, to see that she was gazing at him in mixed horror and alarm.

'Michael, your forehead – the soft spot! It's torn, bleeding, and – *Michael, it's an eye.*'

Slade felt blank. Almost automatically, he bent towards the rearview mirror, tilting it upwards to catch his head. The skin was torn raggedly starting about an inch from the hairline, and coming down about two inches.

A third eye was plainly visible.

The eyelid of it was closed by a surplus of sticky matter, abruptly he grew aware that it was pulsing with a vague perception of light.

It began to hurt.

LOCAL MAN HAS THREE EYES

A car accident, which tore a layer of skin from the fore-head of Michael Slade yesterday, revealed that the young business executive has three eyes. Mr. Slade, when interviewed in the hospital, where he was taken by a passing motorist, seemed in good spirits, but could offer no reason for his possession of a third eye. 'I always had that soft spot in my forehead,' he said. 'The eye itself seems to be a thoroughly useless appendage. I can't imagine Nature's purpose.'

He admitted that it was very likely that he would have the skin grafted into place again. 'People,' he said, 'go to sideshows to see freaks. Otherwise they don't like to look at them.'

The discovery of a three-eyed man in this small city caused a buzz of interest in local scientific circles. At Technical High, Mr. Arthur Trainor, biology teacher, suggested that it was either a mutation, or else that a third eye was once common to human beings, and this is a retrogression. He felt, however, that the latter possibility was controverted by the fact that two eyes were normal throughout the entire animal world. There was, of course, the gland known as the pineal eye.

Dr. Joseph McIver, eye specialist, thought that it would be an interesting experiment to bring all three eyes back to perfect vision. He agreed that this would be difficult, since Mr. Slade's third eye has a bare perception of light, and also because the famous eye training systems now in existence have a hard enough time getting two imperfect eyes back to focus together and work perfectly.

'Nevertheless,' Dr. McIver concluded, 'the human brain is a strange and wonderful machine. When it is relaxed, everything balances. But when it is tensed for any reason, eye, ear, stomach and other organic troubles begin.'

Mrs. Slade, whom our reporter tried to interview, could not be reached.

BEFORE THE CORONER'S JURY
STATEMENT OF MRS. M. SLADE

My name is Miriam Leona Crenshaw. I am the former Mrs. Michael Slade. I divorced Mr. Slade and have legal right to use my maiden name. I met Michael Slade about six years ago, and had no suspicion that he was anything but a normal individual.

I saw my husband only twice after the car accident that revealed his abnormality. The first time it was to plead with him to change his mind about keeping all his three eyes visible. But he had been profoundly influenced by a comment in the press by a local eye specialist concerning the possibility that he might recover the vision of his three eyes. And he felt that publicity had then been so widespread that any attempt at deception was useless.

This determination was the sole reason for our separation, and it was to sign the separation papers that I saw him the second time.

I know nothing special of subsequent events. I did not even look at the body. Its crushed condition having been described to me, I refused to view it.

Slade sat palming and glancing at the Snellen charts, waiting for the eye specialist.

The sun was shining down on the chart, but he himself was in shadow, and comfortably ensconced in an easy-chair. Relaxation, that was the secret.

Only, after nearly three months of doing it on his own from books, his progress had been comparatively tiny.

Footsteps crunched on the walk. Slade looked up at the eye specialist curiously. Dr. McIver was a tall gray-haired man of fifty-five or so; that much was visible to Slade without glasses.

The doctor said : 'Your man told me I would find you here.'

He did not wait for a reply, but stood at ease, looking across the lawn at the three charts, respectively five, ten and twenty feet from the chair in which Slade sat.

'Well,' he said, 'I see you're familiar with the principles of eye training. I wish a billion more people would realize how satisfactory it is to have a light of ten thousand candle-power shining from the sky into their back yards. I think,' he confided, 'before I die I shall become a sun worshipper!'

Slade found himself warming to the man. He had been a little doubtful, when he had phoned Dr. McIver, about inviting even a specialist into his problem. But his doubts began to fade.

He explained his trouble. After nearly three months his third eye could see the ten-foot line at one foot, but with each additional foot that he drew back from the chart, its vision became worse out of all proportion to the extra distance. At three feet he could barely see the two hundred foot C.

'In other words,' Dr. McIver said, 'it's largely mental now. Your mind is suppressing images with which it is familiar, and you can be almost certain that it is suppressing them because it has been in the habit of doing so.'

He turned, and began to unpack his bag. 'Let's see,' he said confidently, 'if we can't persuade it to give in.'

Slade could literally feel himself relaxing before the glowing positivities of this man. This was what he needed. For long now, tensions must have been building up inside him. Unconsciously he must be resenting his slow progress.

'A few questions first,' said Dr. McIver, straightening with a retinascope in his hand : 'Have you been reading fine print every day ? Can you "swing" the letters? Have you accustomed your eyes to direct sunlight? O.K. ! Let's begin with the right eye without palming.'

Slade was able to read at twenty feet the line that should have been visible at fifty. He was aware of McIver standing eight feet away studying his eye through the retinascope. The eye specialist nodded finally.

'Vision of right eye 20/50. Astigmatism of two diopters.' He added : 'Do you practise looking at dominoes ?'

Slade nodded. Up to a point he had made considerable progress with the muscle imbalance that caused the astigmatism which affected all three of his eyes.

'Left eye next,' said Dr. McIver. And a little later : 'Vision 20/70, astigmatism of three diopters.'

'Center eye, vision 3/200, astigmatism of 11 diopters. Now palm.'

Palming produced long flashes of 20/20 vision in his right and left eyes, and a bare instant of 5/70 vision in his centre eye.

'I think,' said Dr. McIver, 'we shall start by trying for a better illusion of black. What you see may seem black to your imagination, but you're fooling yourself. Afterwards, we'll do some whipping and shifting, and bounce a few tennis balls.'

He fumbled in his bag, and came up with a roll of black materials. Slade recognised a black fur piece, black wool, black cotton, a square of black cardboard, black silk, a piece of black metal, a hand-engraved ebony ornament, and a variety of familiar black items including a plastic fountain pen, a bow tie, and a small book with a black cover.

'Look them over,' McIver said. 'The mind cannot remember any shade of black more than a few seconds. Palm, and switch your imagination from one to the other of these items.'

After half an hour, Slade had improved noticeably the vision of each eye. He could see the large C with his third eye at twenty feet, and the R and B below it were recognisable blurs. But perfect vision was still a long, long way off.

'Again, palm,' said Dr. McIver. This time he went on talking softly as Slade closed his eyes. 'Black is black is black. There is no black but black. Black, pure, unadulterated black is black black.'

It was nonsense with a pattern of reason in it. Slade found himself smiling, as he visualised the black in the various articles that McIver had placed on his lap. Black, he thought, black, wherefore art thou, black?

As simply as that it came. Black as black as the black of a moonless, starless night, black as printer's ink, black as all the black that the mind of man ever conceived. The black.

He opened his center eye, and saw the ten line on the twenty-foot chart. He blinked, but it was still there as bright and black as the print itself. Startled, he opened the other two eyes. And still there was no blurring. With 20/10 vision in all three of his eyes he looked around his back yard.

He *saw!*

At first, the fence and the other residences and the charts and all the shrubbery remained as a part of the scene. It was like looking at two pictures, with one super-imposed upon the other, like two images coming through two different sets of eyes. But images of different scenes.

The familiar one – his own back yard, and the hill to the right and the rooftops of his neighbours that made up his horizon – had the effect of blurring the other, stranger scene.

Gradually, however, its outlines pushed through. To his left, where the houses fell away into a large shallow depression, was an enormous expanse of marsh, thick with brilliant growth. To his right, where the hill had always hidden his view, were scores of caves with fires burning at their openings.

The smoke from the fires rose up in curling tongues of black and grey, intensified the blur that already half hid the Morton and Gladwander mansions, which dominated the hill. They kept fading, fading. And now, Slade saw that the hill with the caves was somewhat higher and steeper than the hill with the houses. There was a wide ledge that ran along in front of the caves. And it was on this ledge that he suddenly noticed something else.

Human beings! They moved around, now bending over pots that hung above the fires, now adding wood to the fires, or disappearing into the caves, and then emerging again. There were not many, and most of them had long hair characteristic of woman, or else they were small and child-like. Their primitive clothes – clearly visible even at this distance – made the reality of them unnatural.

Slade sat there. He had a remote impulse to get up, but it was too soon yet for reaction or even understanding. At last memory came that this was happening as a result of improvement in his vision; and the lightning thought followed : What in the name of sanity had happened?

It was too vague as yet, that tugging amazement, and besides there was still the scene of the cave dwellers becoming clearer and clearer to his vision. The houses and his own yard were just shimmering images, like fading mirages, like things dimly seen through an all-enveloping haze.

For the first time Slade realised that his eyes had been straining to hold those two scenes, but that the strain was lessening, as the second one took stronger and stronger hold of his attention.

The paralysis left him. Quite automatically, he stood up.

He noted, with enormous and developing interest, that, where the marsh ended, a rolling meadow began, spotted here and there with bright splashes of gigantic flowering shrubs, and in the distance trees that looked amazingly tall.

Everything was as clear and bright as a summer sun could make it. A warm, glowing wilderness, almost untouched by man, spread before him. It was like a fairy land, and he stared.

At last, with wondering delight, he turned to look at the

other horizon – and the girl must have started the same instant around the tree that was there.

She was tall and very straight. She must have been intending to swim in the stream that babbled into the marsh a few yards away because, except for a rather ornamental silvery belt around her waist, she had no clothes on.

She had three eyes, and all three of them appraised Slade with amazement but without a shade of embarrassment. There was something else in her manner that was not so prepossessing, even a little repellent. It was the dominating look of a woman accustomed to think only of herself. He had time to realise that she was older than she looked.

The woman's eyes were narrowing. She spoke in a violin-toned contralto, meaningless words, but offensively sharp in tone.

She began to fade. The trees, the great marsh, the hill, partly visible to his left now, faded perceptibly. A house showed through her body, and all around, the earth as he had known it for years took swift form.

Suddenly, there was the yard, and himself standing beside his chair. There was Dr. McIver, his back to Slade, peering around the corner of the house. The eye specialist turned, and his face lighted as he saw Slade.

'Where did you go?' he asked. 'I turned my back, and you're off without a word.'

Slade made no immediate reply. The pain in his eyes was like a fire.

It burned and burned.

BEFORE THE CORONER'S JURY
STATEMENT OF DR. McIVER

I had personal contact with Michael Slade over a period of about two and half months. For an hour a day I assisted him with his eye training. It was a slow process, as, after apparently recovering the first day, he had an unusually sharp retrogression.

When I asked him about any particular effects he had observed during his brief spell of good vision he hesitated a long time, and then shook his head.

At the end of ten weeks his third eye had a normal vision of only 10/400. He decided then that he was going to take a holiday on his farm at Canonville, in the hope that his childhood surroundings would relax his mind, and so effect a cure.

I understand he later returned to his home, but I did not see him again until I was called to identify his smashed body in the morgue.

CHAPTER TWO

The first day on the farm! It was distinctly cooler. A September breeze was blowing over the pasture, when Slade settled down with his eye charts. He glanced at the sun, already low in the west, for he had arrived late. And he sighed. The day was almost gone.

It had to be today. That feeling was strong in him. This afternoon he was still convinced that it would be easy to recall the relaxed days of his childhood on the farm. By tomorrow, if he failed today, the tension of doubt would have set in.

Then, too, there had been the anxious feeling way in the back of his mind about the cave dwellers. He was just a little reluctant to appear within a stone's throw of a primitive tribe. Here, on this prairie, it was different. It was very unlikely that any inhabitants of that obviously sparsely settled world would be anywhere in the vicinity.

What the mind wants to see, Slade thought, *it will see if it is there to see.* He was creating conditions where his mind would again want to see.

He palmed, and then looked at the chart with his centre eye. He could see the big C at twenty feet; the R and B below it were a blur, and the T F P a blotch of gray. As an improvement it was practically worthless.

He palmed again. The eyeball, according to the eye training theorists, was a round organ, which elongated for near vision, and flattened for distance vision. Some of the practitioners were willing to concede the possibility that the ciliary muscles did, in addition, change to some extent the shape of the lens.

But whatever the explanation behind the reality that the system worked, if the muscles pulled disproportionately, vision was poor. The fact that those muscles were controlled by the imagination, a difficult part of the mind to train, made the problem all the more intricate for people who had long worn glasses or had eye trouble.

The solution, Slade thought, *is in me. I have got rid of all the astigmatism in my right or left eye, yet my center eye persists in being astigmatic, sometimes to the point of blindness.*

It was of the mind, his trouble. His eye had proved that it was able to function normally.

About an hour before sundown, his brain was still refusing to work with the third eye.

Perhaps, Slade thought, *if I went to the various spots, of which I have particularly vivid childhood memories, I'd be able to recapture the mood and –*

First, the creek beside which he had hidden so often in the brush, and watched the cars go by to their remote and wonderful destinations.

The grass had grown deep where he had once worn it down with his small body. He knelt, and the scent was a tang in his nostrils. He pressed his face to the cool, green softness of it, and he lay quiet, conscious of his weariness and of the sustained effort he had made during the past months.

Am I a fool? he wondered. *Did I turn my wife against me, break off with my friends, all in order to follow a will-o'-the-wisp?*

And had he really seen that other world, or was that some fantastic illusion which his mind had experienced during a profound organic readjustment?

His mood of depression intensified. The sun went down, and twilight was yielding to darkness when he finally started back along the bank of the creek towards the farmhouse.

In the darkness he couldn't find the path, and so he struck across the pasture, stumbling once in a while through thicker patches of grass. He could see the light of the end window of the farmhouse, but it seemed farther away than he remembered. The first alarm came with that realisation, but it wasn't until five minutes later that a far more telling fear struck into him. The fence! He should have come to the fence long ago.

The light seemed to be only a few hundred feet from where he stopped short.

Slade sank slowly down onto the grass. He swallowed hard and then he thought : *This is ridiculous. I'm imagining things.*

But there was an empty sensation in the pit of his stomach, as he strove to penetrate the intense darkness all around him. There was no moon, and clouds must have been heavy overhead, for not a single star showed. The light in the near distance glowed with a hazy but bright steadiness. It failed, however, to illuminate the building from which it came.

Slade blinked at it with a gathering fascination, his tense-ness draining before the consciousness that it would probably be easy to get back to Earth. After all, he had *thought* himself here. He should be able to get back without too much trouble.

He climbed to his feet, and began to walk forward. As the light drew nearer, it seemed to him that it was coming from inside a doorway. Vaguely, he could make out that the doorway was inset under a curving sweep of metal, that bulged far out. The metal gleamed dully, and then merged with the general blackness without leaving a hint of the shape of the whole structure.

Slade hesitated about a hundred feet from the entrance. He was even more fascinated than he had been, but his desire to investigate was dwindling. Not now, in this dark night of a strange plane of existence. Wait till morning. And yet he had the uneasy conviction that before dawn the tensions would have reasserted in his mind.

One knock at the door, he thought, *one look inside. And then off into the darkness.* The door was metal, and so solid that his knuckles made only the vaguest sound. He had some silver coins in his pocket, and they tinged with a sharp sound as he used them. Instantly, he stepped back, and waited.

The silence grew tremendous, like a pall pushing at him. Dark and silent night in a primitive land inhabited by cave-men and –

And what? This was no caveman's residence. Was it possible he had come to a plane of Earth entirely separate from that of the nude girl he had seen?

He retreated into the shadows away from the light. He stumbled, barking his shins. On one knee, he felt the object over which he had nearly fallen. Metal. That brought a thrill of real interest. Cautiously, he pressed the button of his flashlight, but it wouldn't light. Slade cursed under his breath, and tugged at the metal thing in the ground. That was the trouble. It was in the ground. And held hard.

It seemed to be a wheel attached to a boxing of some kind. He was still fumbling over it, tugging tentatively, when it began to rain. That sent him to the nearest brush for cover. But the rain grew heavier, until finally the bush poured water on him. Slade accepted his fate, and headed back for the doorway. He tried the latch, and pushed. The door opened immediately.

The interior was brightly lighted, a long, high wide corridor of dully shining metal. About a hundred feet away, the massive hallway ended in a cross corridor. There were three doorways on each side of the corridor.

He tried the doors one after another. The first one opened into a long, narrow room that was all shiny blue mirror. At least it looked like a mirror. Then he grew aware that stars were shining in its depth.

Slade closed the door hastily. It wasn't that he felt fear. But his mind had hesitated, unable to interpret what it was seeing. Its hold on this world was far too precarious for him to subject it to incomprehensible strangeness.

He moved across the hall to the first door on his left. It opened onto a long, narrow room half filled with case on case of goods. Some of them were open, their contents spilled out on the floor. Instruments glittered up at him, a quantity array of miscellaneous gadgets of all sizes. Some of the boxes were haphazardly pulled aside, as if a searcher had been looking for some specific item.

Slade closed that door too, puzzled but without any threatening strain this time. A storeroom was a recognisable thing, and his mind accepted it without there being any necessity for him to identify what was in the boxes.

The two middle doors revealed identical interiors. Massive machines that towered three quarters of the way to the ceiling. In spite of their size Slade recognised them for what they were. For more than a year American papers and magazines had shown pictures of the atomic engine developed at the University of Chicago for rocket ships. The design was slightly different, but the general tenor was unmistakable.

Slade closed each door in turn, hastily. And stood in the hallway, dissatisfied with the situation. A spaceship settled on a lonely moor in an alien plane of existence brilliantly lighted inside, and a solitary light outside like a beacon in the night beckoning to wanderers like himself, offering surcease from the darkness – was that the reality?

Slade doubted it, and a grisly feeling came that he had

willed himself into a nightmare, and that any instant he would wake up, perspiring, in his bed.

But the instants passed, and there was no waking. Gradually, his mind accepted the silence, the brief panic faded, and he tried the fifth door.

It opened into darkness. Slade stepped back hastily. His eyes grew accustomed to the shadows, and so after scant seconds he saw the shape. It was pressed against the darkest wall, and it watched him alertly from three eyes that gleamed brightly in the vaguely reflected light. One swift look Slade had, and then his mind refused the vision.

Instantly, the ship, the light, vanished. He fell about three feet to a grassy embankment. Half a mile away was a yellow glowing light. It turned out to be his own farmhouse.

He was back on Earth.

Slade remained on the farm, undecided. The vision of all three of his eyes had deteriorated this time, and besides he was a badly shaken man. It couldn't have been the same woman, he told himself. Standing there in the shadows of a corridor of an old, seemingly deserted spaceship, the same young woman – watching him.

And yet, the resemblance to the nude cave girl had been so apparent to his brain that he had instantly been under an abnormal strain. His mind proved that it recognised her by the speed with which it *rejected* the logic of her presence.

The question was, should he continue his exercises? For a whole month he walked the reaches of the farm, unable to make up his mind. And the main reason for his indecision was his realisation that his return to the two-eyed world had not been absolutely necessary.

Normal vision was a product of many balancing factors, not only mental but physical. Muscles weakened by glasses or by disuse lacked the endurance to resist the shudderingly swift impulses of the mind. Properly strengthened, they would withstand far greater shocks than he had experienced.

A demonic woman, he thought, *standing in the shadows of a shadow ship in a shadow land.* He was no longer sure he wanted to commit himself to that other plane of existence – to a woman who was aware of him, and who was trying to lure him.

After a month, the first snowfall whitened the foothills. Still undecided, Slade returned to the city.

My name is Ernest Gray, and I am a professor of languages. Some time ago – I cannot remember the exact date – I received a visit from Michael Slade. It seems that he had been away on his farm, and that, on returning to his city home, he learned that, in his absence, a three-eyed woman had visited his home.

From the account Mr. Slade gave me, I understand that his manservant admitted the woman to the house – she seems to have been a very assured and dominating individual – and permitted her to remain five days as a guest. At the end of that time, the day before Mr. Slade's return, she departed leaving behind her nearly a score of phonograph records and a letter. Mr. Slade showed me the letter. Although it is to be shown to the jury as a separate exhibit, I am herewith including it in my statement to clarify my own account. The letter read as follows:

Dear Mr. Slade:

I want you to use the phonograph records to learn the language of Naze. The key record will dissolve in about two weeks after it is first played, but during that time it should have helped you to gain complete mastery of Nazia.

The situation on Naze is very simple, as you will discover, but it is also very dangerous. Here is what you must do. As soon as you have learned the language, drive to the plateau two miles west of the city of Smailes, and park your car beside an abandoned granary several hundred yards from the road at midnight of any night.

In all your ventures on Naze, beware of Geean and the hunters of the city.

Leear.

By the time Mr. Slade brought the records to me, the key record had dissolved, but after listening to those that remained I am able to say without qualification that the language is a fraud, possibly an artificial creation of the three-eyed people for secret intercommunication.

I am assuming, now that a three-eyed woman has turned up, that there is more than one three-eyed freak in the world. My first reaction was that the name, Naze, might have some connection to the Nazi party, but the pronunciation of the word as given in the records, rhymes with faze and daze.

It is unfortunate that the key record was destroyed. Without such a key there can be no translation of a language which, in the ultimate issue, is nothing but a product of the imagination of three-eyed neurotics.

I am told that Mr. Slade's body was found near the city of Smailes, about a mile from the granary outhouse referred to in the letter of the woman Leear. But I know nothing about that, and did not myself see the body.

CHAPTER THREE

At first Slade sat in the car. But as midnight drew near, he climbed out and examined the granary with the probing beam of his flashlight. The bare, unpainted interior was as empty as it had been in the afternoon when he had driven out for an exploratory look.

The stubble field stretched off into darkness beyond the farthest ray of his flash. A quarter moon rode the eastern sky, and the stars shone with a pale radiance, but the resulting light failed to make his surroundings visible.

Slade glanced at his watch. And though he had known the hour was near, he felt a shock. 11:55. In five minutes, he thought shakily, *she* would come.

Not for the first time, he regretted his presence. Was he a fool, he wondered, to come here – risk himself on an abandoned farm, where his loudest shouts for help would merely echo mockingly from the near hills? He had a gun of course, but he knew that he would hesitate to use it.

He shook himself. She had been cunning, had the woman Leear, not naming a date for him to come. *Any* midnight, she had said. She must have known that that would work and work on the mind of the only three-eyed man of Earth. If she had named a time as well as a place, he could have made up his mind against it.

The indefiniteness nullified his resistance. Each day that passed brought the same problem: Would he go tonight? Or wouldn't he? Each day, the pro and con, with all its emotional overtones, racked his mind and body. And in the end he decided that she wouldn't have taught him the language of Naze in order to harm him in the night that he came to keep their rendezvous.

She was interested in him. What she wanted was something else again, but being what he was, a three-eyed man, he could not but be interested in her. If talking to her tonight would bring him information, then the risk was more than justified.

Here he was, for better or worse.

Slade put away his flash, and glanced at the illuminated dials of his watch. Once again, but even more tinglingly, the shock ran down his spine. It was exactly midnight.

The silence was intense. Not a sound penetrated the night. He had turned off the headlights of his car. Now, abruptly, it seemed to him that he had made a mistake. The lights should be on.

He started towards the car, and then stopped. What was the matter with him? This was no time to desert the shelter of the granary. He backed slowly until his body touched the wall. He stood there fingering his gun. He waited.

The sound that came to him there was almost not a sound at all. The air, which had been quiet, was suddenly gently agitated. But the breeze was not normal. It came from above.

From above! With a jerk, Slade looked up. But he saw nothing. Not a movement was visible against the dark, dark-blue of the sky. He felt a thrill akin to fire, a sense of the unknown stronger than anything he had ever experienced, and then –

'The important thing, Michael Slade,' said the resonant, familiar voice of Leear from the air almost directly above him, 'is for you to stay alive during the next twenty-four hours while you are in the city of Naze. Be cautious, sensible, and make no unnecessary admissions about what you do or do not know. Good luck.'

There was a dazzling flash of light from about a dozen feet above. Slade blinked, and snatched his gun. Then he stood tensed, and looked around wildly.

The granary was gone, and his car, and the stubble field. He was on a city street. Buildings loomed darkly all around him, spirelike shapes that reared up towards a haze of violet light which half-hid the night sky beyond. The light spread like a great curving dome from an enormously high spire in the distance.

Slade saw those details in one flashing glance. Even as he looked, understanding came of what had happened. He had been transported to the city of Naze.

At first the street seemed deserted, the silence utter. But then, swiftly, his senses began to adjust. He heard a vague sound, as if somebody had whispered to somebody else. Far along the street, a shadowed figure raced across the road, and vanished into the darkness beside a spire.

It struck Slade with a pang that his position here in the center of the street put him at a disadvantage. He began to edge carefully towards the sidewalk to the right. The road-bed was uneven, and twice he stumbled and almost fell. The greater darkness under a tree enveloped him, and he had barely reached it when there was a human screech about fifty yards away.

The sound was jarring. With a spasmodic movement, Slade flung himself onto the ground, simultaneously raising his gun. He lay very still. He waited.

It took a moment for his brain to gather together. And several seconds passed before he could locate the direction of what was now a noisy struggle. Cries and groans and muffled shouts came from the darkness. They ended abruptly, and there followed a curious silence. It was as if the assailants had been worn out by their struggle and were now resting. Or – what was more likely – they were silently and greedily engaged in searching their victim.

Slade's brain had time to catch up with his reflexes. His first thought had in it a blank, amazed quality. What had he run into? He lay quiet, clutching his automatic tightly, and after a moment the second thought came: So this was the city of Naze.

Briefly, then, he felt overwhelmed. He thought. *How did she do it? How did she transfer me here?* There had been, he remembered, a flash of light. And instantly he was in Naze.

She must have used the same mechanical means as she had employed to transfer to the Earth plane. An instrument the light of which somehow affected the visual center behind each eye. There seemed no other logical explanation, and that logic, with the spaceship as an additional example, pointed to a highly developed science, that included a thorough understanding of the human nervous system.

The question was, would the effect of the light be perma-nent? Or would it wear off?   –

His thought was interrupted by a cry of rage. 'Give us our share of the blood, you dirty –'

The words were shouted in the language of Naze, and Slade understood them all except the last one. It was that instantaneous, easy comprehension that thrilled him for a moment. Then the meaning penetrated also. Blood. Share of the blood.

Lying there, it seemed to Slade that he must have mis-understood. His doubt ended as another, even more furious cry came, this from a second voice:

'The thief has a double-sized container. He got twice as much blood as the rest of us.'

A third voice, obviously that of the accused, shouted, 'It's a lie.' The man must have recognised that his denial would not be accepted. Footsteps came racing along the street. A tall man, breathing hard, flung himself past Slade. Rushing after him, and strung out behind him, came four other men, all smaller than the first.

They charged past where Slade was lying, vague, manlike shapes that quickly vanished into the night. For nearly a minute he could hear the noise their feet made, and once there was a loud curse.

The sound faded as had the sight. There was silence. Slade did not move. He was realising the full import of what he had seen and heard. A dead man, drained of blood, must be lying on the street a few hundred feet away. Realising – Naze at night was a city of vampires.

A minute, two minutes, dragged by. The thought came to Slade, *But what am I supposed to do? What am I here for?*

He recalled what the woman Leear had told him just before she flashed the light at him. 'The important thing, Michael Slade, is for you to remain alive during the next twenty-four hours while you are in the city of Naze.'

Twenty-four hours! Slade felt a chill. Was he expected to remain in Naze for an entire day and night with no other instructions but that he remain alive? No purpose, no place to go, nothing but – this!

If only there were street lights. But he could see none in any direction. Not that it was pitch dark. An alien shining-ness glowed at him, different from the night-lit cities of Earth. The sky glowed palely where the violet haze trailed down from the central tower, and lights flickered from the slitted windows of a dozen spires that he could see.

It was definitely not pitch dark, and in a way that might be to his advantage. It seemed clear that he couldn't continue to lie where he was. And darkness would provide protection for an uneasy explorer.

He climbed to his feet, and he was about to step from under the tree when a woman called softly to him from across the street:

'Mr. Slade.'

Slade froze. Then he half turned. And then he recognised

that he had been addressed by name. His relief left him weak.

'Here!' he whispered loudly. 'Here!'

The woman came across the street. 'I'm sorry I'm late,' she whispered breathlessly, 'but there are so many blood seekers abroad. Follow me.' Her three eyes gleamed at him. Then she turned, and headed rapidly up the street. And it was not until Slade was swinging along behind her that the startling realisation came to him that this woman was not Leear.

Swiftly, he and his guide headed deeper into the city.

They climbed one of the darkest stairways Slade had ever seen, then paused before a door. The girl knocked, a measured knock. Three times slow, two fast, and then after a short interval, one.

The pause was long. While they waited, the girl said:

'Mr. Slade, we all want to thank you for coming – for the risks you are taking. We will do our best to familiarise you with Naze. Let us hope that this time the ship will be able to destroy the city.'

'Uh!' said Slade.

The exclamation could have been a giveaway, but at last the instant he had an awareness of the danger of his surprise. He choked the sound down to a contorted whisper.

There was the click of a lock. The door creaked open. Light poured out into the hallway. It revealed a heavily built woman slowly making her way to a chair.

Inside, Slade examined his surroundings. The room was both long and wide. For its size, it was scantily furnished. There were three settees and two lounges, end tables, tables, chairs and rugs. The drapes could once have belonged to his divorced wife, Miriam.

Once? A very long time ago, Slade decided after a second glance. They looked as if they had originally cost a great deal. They were so shabby now that they actually seemed out of place.

Slade let the room recede into the background of his tired mind. He walked over, and sat down in a chair, facing the older woman; but it was the younger woman he looked at.

She paused a few feet away, and was now standing smiling at him. She was a lean, olive-complexioned girl with a proud smile.

Slade said: 'Thank you for the risks *you* took.'

The girl shook her head with an easy smile. 'You'll be

wanting to go to bed. But first I want you to meet Caldra, the Planner. Caldra, this is Slade of the ship.'

There it was, definite, stated. Of the ship, He, Michael Slade! Leear was certainly taking a great deal for granted.

The older woman was looking at him with strange, slow eyes. The impression of slowness was so distinct that Slade looked at her sharply for the first time. Her eyes were the colour of lead, her face colourless, pasty, unnatural. Lusterless, almost lifeless, she stared at him. And said in a dead slow voice:

'Mr. Slade, it is a pleasure.'

It was not a pleasure to Slade. He had to strain to keep the repelled look off his face. Once, perhaps twice, before in his life, people had affected him like this, but neither of the other two had matched this creature for the unpleasant sensation they made him feel.

Slow thyroid, he analysed. The identification made her presence more palatable to his soul. It freed his mind. Memory came of what the girl had called the other. His brain paused. Caldra, the Planner.

He relaxed slowly, and made a conscious concession. She might be very good at that. Slow brains could be extremely thorough.

His interest began to sink. The strain of his experiences weighed suddenly on him. In his teens and early twenties, he had been a night hound, a haunter of cocktail bars and clubs. At thirty he had started to go to bed at ten o'clock, much to Miriam's disgust. Midnight usually found him yawning and sleepy. And here it was – he glanced at his watch – five minutes to one. He glanced at the girl. He said:

'I can use that bed.'

As the girl led him towards a corridor door, the older woman mumbled:

'Things are shaping up. Soon, the hour of decision will be upon us.' Just as Slade went out of the door, she said something else with the faintest suggestion of a laugh. It sounded like, 'Don't get too near him, Amor. I felt it, too.'

The words seemed meaningless. But he was surprised, as the girl opened the bedroom door, to notice that the colour in her cheeks was high. But all she said was:

'You're reasonably safe here. There is a very large group of us who believe in the destruction of Naze, and this is our port of the city.'

In spite of his weariness, a gathering excitement kept Slade awake. He had been too tense to realise his situation. The thoughts that had come were simply the first unfoldings of his mind. But now, in bed, slowly relaxing, the tremendousness of what was happening penetrated.

He was in Naze. Outside the walls of this building was a fantastic city of another plane of existence. And tomorrow he would see that city in all its strangeness. Tomorrow!

He slept.

CHAPTER FOUR

Naze seen under a brilliant morning sun was a jarring spectacle. Slade walked beside Amor along a wide street. Shabby city, he thought, distressed. And old, oh, old!

He had realised the night before that Naze was ancient and decadent. But he hadn't grasped the extent of the disaster that had befallen the city. The buildings that he saw looked older than all his imaginings. Five hundred, perhaps even a thousand years had dragged by since those buildings were built.

For hundreds of thousands of days and nights, the city had rotated under its sun. Its streets and sidewalks had borne the load of daily living. The strangest building materials could not but be worn out after such a lapse of time. And they were.

The sidewalks were almost uniformly rubble, with only here and there a patch of smooth hardness to show what the original had been like. The streets were a little better, but they, too, were largely dust packed down by the pressures that had been put on them.

Not a single vehicle was visible anywhere, only people, people and more people. Evidently, all wheel machines had long ago been worn out.

What had happened? What *could* have happened? There was, of course, the war between the city and the ship – but why? He half-turned to the girl to ask the question, then abruptly remembered that it would be unwise to show ignorance. Leear had warned him to make no admissions.

The city that surrounded him, so obvious a relic of an ancient culture, drained the fever of that fire out of him. Never anywhere had he seen so many people on the streets of a metropolis. With this difference. These people weren't going anywhere. Men and women sat on the curbs, on the sidewalks and on the roads. They seemed unmindful of individuals who brushed past them. They sat, staring vaguely into nothingness. The mindlessness of it was awful to see.

A beggar fell into step beside Slade. He held up a metal cup:

'A few drops of your blood, mister,' he whined. 'I'll slit your throat if you don't give it to me.'

Amor's whip lashed out, and struck the ghoulish thing in the face. The blow raised a welt on the man's face. Blood trickled from the welt.

'Drink your own blood!' the girl snapped.

Her colour was high, Slade noticed, her face twisted with almost unnatural hatred.

'Those beasts,' she said in a low, intense voice, 'lurk in alleyways at night in gangs, and attack anybody who comes along. But, of course,' she broke off, 'you know all about that.'

Slade made no comment. It was true that he knew of the night gangs, but what he didn't know would fill a book.

The continuing reality tore his mind from that very personal problem. The streets swarmed with people *who had nothing to do*. And again, and again and again, fingers plucked at Slade's sleeve, and avid voices whimpered:

'Your blood is strong, mister. You can spare a little, or else –'

Often and often, it was a woman's face that leered up at him.

Slade was silent. He was so appalled he could have spoken only with difficulty. He looked down side street after side street, boiling with lecherous beings; and he saw for the first time in his life what utter depravity was possible to the human animal.

This city must continue to exist. It was clear now why Leear had lured him into he city. She wanted him to see, and she must believe the actuality would end any doubts in his mind. Doubts, for instance, about the reasons for the immeasurably horrible conditions – unquestionably due to the war between the ship and the city. Understanding the origin of a plague was a side issue.   –

The plague itself must be wiped out.

He had no doubts; so great was his horror. He felt sick with an absolute dismay. This, he thought, going on day after day, year after year, through centuries. It mustn't. The girl was speaking:

'For a while we thought if we could get the chemicalised cups away from them, we could end the blood craze. But –'

She stopped; she shrugged, finished: 'Of course you know

all about that. Except in rare cases, depravity only sinks to new depths; it does not rise.'

There was nothing to say to that. It was easy to see that his NOT knowing 'all about that' was going to be a handicap to his understanding of the details of hell. He didn't really need the details though; the overall hell was enough.

End it! Destroy it! Help the ship if he could, help these fifth columnists. But destroy Naze.

He grew calmer. He analysed her words. Chemicalised cups! Then it wasn't the blood itself, but some chemical in the metal of the cup, that made it so intoxicatingly attractive.

Removal of the cup apparently had channeled the craving into something worse. What? Well, he was supposed to know.

Slade smiled wearily. 'Let's go back,' he said. 'I've had enough for today.'

The early part of the lunch was eaten in silence. Slade ate, thinking about the city, the ship and the cavemen, and of his own part in the affair. In a way he now knew the essentials of the situation. He had seen the ship, and he was seeing the city.

The question was, just what was he supposed to do? He realised abruptly that Caldra, the slow, was about to speak.

The woman was laying down her fork. That movement alone required many seconds. Then she lifted her head. It seemed to Slade that it took her eyes an unnaturally long time to focus upon him.

The next step was even more prolonged. She opened her mouth, sat considering her first sentence, and finally began to articulate the syllables. Over a period that seemed longer than it was, she said:

'Tonight, we raid Geean's central palace. Our forces can guarantee to get you to the fortieth level as agreed. The apparatus Leear asked for is already there, ready to ease you out of the window, so that you can focus your dissembler onto the controls of the barrier. You no doubt saw for yourself when you were out this morning that they are located at about the ninetieth level.

'We assume, of course, that the ship will rush in the moment the barrier is down.'

Long before her measured words reached their end, Slade had grasped their import. He sat motionless, eyes half closed, startled. Tonight. But that was ridiculous. He couldn't be expected to rush into an attack as blindly as that.

His opinion of Leear went down a million miles. What was a dissembler anyway? Surely, he wasn't expected to learn how to operate an intricate mechanism during the heat of a battle. His consternation reached a peak as Caldra fell silent, and looked at him expectantly. Amor, too, he saw, was watching him with eager anticipation.

Slade parted his lips, and then closed them again, as another, greater realisation struck him. The realisation that he had been given an immense amount of information. It was all by implication, but the import was unmistakable.

The haze of light he had seen the night before, radiating from the skyscraper central tower – and which he recalled suddenly had been vaguely visible during his morning walk as a faint mist – that was the barrier. What kind of a barrier? Apparently, a barrier strong enough to keep the spaceship at bay. A barrier of energies potent beyond anything on Earth.

But that meant the city was under siege, and – judging from the decay – had been for hundreds of years.

Slade's mind poised. 'This,' he told himself, 'is ridiculous. How would they live? Where would they get their food? They can't possibly be living on each other's blood.'

He stared down at his plate, but there was very little left. The remnant looked like a vegetable, though it was covered by a sauce or gravy that hid the details. He looked up, a question about the food quivering in his throat – and realised that this was no time for such things. If he was going to prevent a major disaster, he had better say something, and fast. Before he could speak, Amor said:

'One bold surprise attack and' – she smiled with a savage excitement – 'finish!'

For a moment, the play of emotions across her face held Slade's attention. She was quite a deadly creature herself, this tall girl who carried a whip for the vampires of Naze. It was the old story of environment of course. The mind shaped by its physical climate, and in turn shaping the body and the expression of the face, and setting fast the capabilities of the senses.

For the first time it struck him that, if he committed himself to this plane of Earth, here was a sample of the kind of girl he would eventually marry. He looked at her with

118

interest, prepared to pursue the thought further. And then, once more he realised that his mind was striving to escape from its only immediate problem, the attack. Tonight! He said:

'I'm sorry to have to tell you that the ship will not be here tonight.'

Amor was on her feet, her eyes widening. 'But all our plans!' she gasped.

She seemed overcome. She sat down. Beside her, Caldra emerged from her stupor, and showed that Slade's words had finally penetrated.

'No ship!'

Slade said, 'The ship was to signal me this morning.' He felt as if he were sweating, but it was a mental sensation, not a physical one. He went on, 'There was no signal.'

It was not bad, he realised, for ad lib. He relaxed, in spite of not having solved his basic problem. He watched Amor head for the door. She paused on the threshold.

'I'll have to call off the attack.'

The door banged behind her, leaving, after a moment, silence.

Amor having failed to turn up, Caldra and Slade ate dinner shortly before dark.

It was late when Amor came in. She slumped into her chair, and began to pick absently at the food that Caldra set before her. Several times Slade caught her looking at him from under her lashes with speculation. And with something else. He couldn't quite decide what.

Slade decided not to let that disturb him. He walked over to the great window of the living room. He was aware of Amor joining him after a while, but she said nothing; and so he, too, held his peace. He looked out at Naze.

Shadowed Naze, night enveloped. Seen from the spire window, the city drifted quietly into darkness. It seemed almost to glide into the shadows that crept in from the east.

Slade gazed and gazed. At last except for the flickering lights and almost invisible barrier, the darkness was complete.

Realisations came: His was surely the strangest adventure in the history of the human nervous system. Born in the foothills of western United States, brought up on a farm, quickly successful as a broker in a small western city. And now here! Here in this dark, doomed city of a planet the civilisation of which was in desperate straits.

And yet it was not an alien planet; simply another plane revealed to his brain and body because he had three eyes instead of two.

The thrill of excitement that came was connected with his companion. She stood beside him, a woman of that world, young and strong, perhaps still unspoken for by any man.

It was possible. He was sure of that. The marriage state was almost meaningless under present conditions.

It was some time since he had given serious thought to the subject of women. Now, he was fairly easy prey. During the afternoon he had thought of Amor in a very possessive fashion, and his previous realisation – that IF he stayed, he would have to marry a girl of this world – had sharpened.

It was possible that there would be other women on this plane of existence more attractive than she was, but they were far away.

Slade said : 'Amor.'

No answer.

'Amor, what are you planning to do afterwards?'

The girl stirred. 'I shall live in a cave, of course. That is what we must all do.'

Slade hesitated, torn from his line of approach by the implications of her words – *Must* all do! Why? It had not struck him before that Amor and her group accepted the idea of a primitive existence.

He remembered that in a kind of a way, he was trying to make a girl.

'Amor.'

'Slade.'

She seemed not to have heard him, for her tone was not an answer, and showed no awareness that he had spoken.

Slade said, 'What is it?'

'This will sound terrible to you, but I was once a blood drinker.'

It seemed a futile confession. It brought no picture at first; the words themselves made him uneasy, however.

'And so was Caldra. And everybody. I don't think I'm exaggerating. There's never anything like it.'

A picture began to come. And thoughts. Slade licked his suddenly dry lips, repelled.

And still he had no idea what she was getting at.

'It was easier for me to break off,' the girl said, 'and to stay off – until today . . . last night. Slade,' her voice was tiny, 'you have strong blood. I felt it all day.'

Abruptly, he knew where she was heading. He thought of the men and women she had lashed with her whip that morning. In a twisted fashion, those blows had been aimed at her own craving.

'You can't imagine,' Amor was saying, 'what a shock it was to Caldra and me when you said the attack was not tonight. It meant you would be around at least another day. Slade, that was terribly unfair. Leear knew our situation only too well.'

The repulsion was greater. It seemed to Slade that in another moment he would be sick. He said in a low voice:

'You want some of my blood.'

'Just a little.' Her tone had the faintest whine in it. Enough to make vivid a picture of her begging on the streets. Slade felt mentally nauseated.

The thought came that he had no business making any remarks. But he was emotionally past that stage of common sense. This was the girl he had tentatively intended to offer marriage. He said harshly: 'And you were the one who used a whip on the others this morning.'

In the darkness of the room, he heard the sharp intake of her breath. There was a long silence. Then she turned, and her body was a slim, shadowed shape that disappeared into a corridor towards her bedroom.

And so the night that was to be long began.

CHAPTER FIVE

After several hours, Slade still couldn't sleep. He had been unfair to somebody he liked; and it was disturbing.

She had rescued him from almost death, restored his health; and, surely, surely, he could spare her a little of his blood. Out of all the people in this fantastic city, she and her group had fought hardest against the craving that had destroyed the soul of Naze.

It must have been a fight to make the very gods take pity. But he had none. He, supermoralist Michael Slade, the perfect man, had cast stones and created pain.

Actually, the true explanation was worse than that, rooted as it was in his own physical desires. And, besides, it was possible that his blood did *feel* stronger to people who were aware of such things.

In the morning, he would give Amor AND Caldra a half cup of blood. And then, somehow, he must get out of this city, back to Earth if possible, but out in some way. It was already after midnight, and clear, therefore, that the end of the twenty-four hour period, which Leear had mentioned, would not automatically return him to the vicinity of his car, near the city of Smailes.

Why, if it meant nothing, had she mentioned a time limit? He dozed, still thinking about that. And weakened to the realisation that someone was in the room.

He lay rigid, striving to penetrate the darkness. The fear that pressed on him was the ancient fear of a man in a hostile land being stalked in the blackness. His straining eyes caught a movement against the silhouetting wall, a shadowy figure.

A *woman*. Amor. The identification brought a measure of pity.

Poor girl! What deadly hunger that desire for blood was. In a blurred fashion, he had in the back of his mind an intention of using a cup to taste his own blood. But her coming under such desperate circumstances ended that intention for the time being. He was only a normal being. He couldn't afford to be caught in the toils of so potent a drug.

He made an effort to sit up. And couldn't. He was held down by straps.

He lay back, the first annoyance sharpening his temper. It was all very well to feel sorry for her, but this was a pretty raw stunt she was pulling.

He parted his lips to say something scathing. He didn't say it. Memory came that this girl was in a bad way. Let her have her blood.

He wouldn't say a word. In the morning he would pretend that nothing had happened. The determination gave him a temporary satisfaction.

In darkness, the vague movement continued. The girl seemed to be in no hurry. Just as Slade's impatience reached the vanishing point, a thin needle of light pointed down at his left arm. Almost simultaneously a hand came into view. It held a syringe, which it inserted deftly into the largest visible vein. Slade watched, interested, as the blood drew up darkly into the transparent body of the instrument.

The seconds slid by, and still the avid needle strained at him. Slade thought of the eeriness of what was happening, an Earthman in a strange world being bled by a likeable vampire girl in the secret dead of the night.

The picture faded with the passing seconds, too many seconds. Slade said gently:

'Don't you think that's enough?'

For several moments after his words broke the silence, the syringe held steady; and there was no sound. At last, the hand and the syringe jerked slightly in surprise.

It was the time gap between his speech and her reaction that brought to Slade his first understanding of the truth. His gaze fixed for the first time on the hand holding the instrument. It was hard to see in the reflections from that narrow band of light. But seeable it was. And recognisable.

It was a woman's hand. Slade sighed as he stared at it. Here was one more proof that the mind created its own illusions. He, who had had so much experience with that reality, whose very presence in the universe of the three-eyed was a living evidence of the importance of mind over matter, still continued to be fooled.

His mind had jumped to the conclusion that it was Amor who had come to his room. When the hand had first come into the light minutes ago, he had noticed nothing unusual. Now he did.

It was a woman's hand all right, but rather worn. And

not young looking at all. How he could have mistaken it even in the reflected light, was a puzzle.

This was Caldra the mysterious, Caldra the Planner, Caldra who, apparently, was now breaking her blood fast. The realisation came to Slade that he was participating in a personal tragedy. A woman whose craving for blood had once nearly destroyed her was drinking blood again.

He was aware of the syringe being withdrawn from his arm. The light winked out. A pause. The sound of thick liquid squirting heavily into a container came next, and then once more silence.

Slade pictured the hand slowly raising the cup towards the fumbling lips. His timing was perfect. As his mental picture of her hand reached her lips, there came an audible gulping.

The sound made Slade a little sick. But pity came too. The emotion died, as fingers touched the bed. He thought with a scowl: More?

But it was the straps that let go their constricting hold on his chest and arms. Footsteps shuffled towards the door, which closed softly.

Silence settled. After a little, Slade slept. When he wakened, a great paw was pressing down on his mouth, and a beast as big as a bear, but with oddly catlike features, was looming over him. Its strong, big, hairy body was illumined by a light held by men in uniform.

Other uniformed men were holding Slade's arms and legs. And he had a dismaying glimpse of still more men in the corridor outside the bedroom.

The animal's great paw withdrew from his face. He was lifted, and carried. There was a light in the living room. He saw Caldra lying face down on the floor, a knife driven to the hilt into her back.

Slade had a horrible, empty sensation. Amor! What about Amor?

It was that thought that must have done it. Under him, the floor dissolved as if it were made of nothingness. He fell about fifteen feet, and struck hard. He lay dizzily for more than a minute before understanding came.

He raised himself slowly, scratching his hands on the frozen stubble of wheat field. About two miles to the west the lights of the city of Smailes blazoned the night sky. Slade climbed to his feet, and headed for the granary where he had left his car. It was still there, silent and lightless.

He waited a few minutes, but there was no sign of Leear. Tired though he was, he drove all the rest of that night, and part of the next morning. It was 11:00 a.m. when he turned up his private drive.

A letter was in the mailbox, in the familiar, masculine handwriting of Leear. Slade frowned at it, then tore it open. It read:

Dear Michael Slade:

Now you know. You have seen Naze. You must have wondered why nothing happened at the exact end of the twenty-four hours. Nothing could happen until after that time, and then only if you received a sufficiently strong shock.

This shock, of course, was provided when one of the women came in and attempted to obtain some of your blood. It was regrettable that such a situation had to be forced, but there was no alternative.

It was unfortunate, too, that I had to let the group in Naze think that there would be an attack. They have no conception of the kind of man they are fighting. Against the immortal Geean, any plan of theirs would fail automatically. Their inability to understand the nature and strength of the enemy is proved by the fact that they accepted without question that the barrier could be destroyed by an attack with a so-called dissembler on a protuberance at the ninetieth floor of the central tower of Geean.

There is no such instrument as a dissembler, and the protuberance on the tower is a radiator. Geean will never be defeated except by an attack into the heart of his stronghold. Such an attack cannot be made without your help, and this time you must come by yourself, as the device which I used beside the granary has only temporary effects.

Do not wait too long.

Leear.

In the daytime, he read and remained within the limits of his yard. At night, hat pulled low over his third eye, head hunched down into the collar of his overcoat, he walked the frozen streets. Slowly, the fever went out of him, and he became grimly sardonic in his attitude to what had happened.

'I am not,' he decided, 'the stuff of which heroes are made. And I have no desire to get killed in the war between Naze and the ship.'

He had better adjust himself to the idea of remaining on this earth.

The half decision made it possible for him to consider Leear's letter from a less emotional viewpoint than when he had first read it. The rereading after three weeks was even more interesting than he had expected, now that his lips did not tighten with anger at the ruthless way Leear had precipitated him into Naze, and so, callously, caused the death of Amor and Caldra.

The letter was basically far less irritating than he had thought. And it certainly lacked the commanding tone that he somehow expected from her. In addition, her frank admission that his help was necessary mollified Slade tremendously.

He was vaguely pleased, too, that she had underestimated him. Her analysis of the kind of shock that would send him back to Earth had been wrong. Caldra coming for blood had scarcely ruffled his nerves. And it had taken the sight of her dead body and a mental picture of Amor similarly murdered to affect him.

After three weeks, he felt himself immune to shock. Caldra and Amor began to seem just a little unreal, like figments of a dream. Slade knew that he had come a long way out of a dangerous mental state when he could think of Amor and feel satiric about his impulse to ask her to marry him.

He did not feel contemptuous of the emotions involved. They were human basics, and it struck him that it might be a sound idea to marry again right here on Earth. If he could persuade Miriam to come and live with him again, that would be a decisive act not easily overthrown by any sudden impulse to rush off to that other plane of existence.

He must resume old relationships, return to a normal Earth existence.

It was easier decided than done. One night, while he was still planning the proper approach to make to Miriam, he met two friends of his business days. They nodded and hurried past, and stopped only when he turned and called after them. The conversation that followed was one of those lame, horrible affairs but Slade was persistent. It seemed to him in his dogged frame of mind that if he was going to live on Earth, he had to have friends and a wife. Those were the concomitants of a sane existence, and he knew better than even to attempt to do without them.

Slade did not enjoy the conversation any more than the two men. They were by turns uneasy, jocular, unhappily silent, eager to impart information, and finally, they hurried off with a 'Glad to have met you, Mike, but we're late now for an engagement. Be seeing you.'

Slade walked home his lips curling ironically, but there was a vague chill in his backbone. He had learned, among other things, that Miriam had had a 'new' boy friend for several months, and there was something strangely final about that fact. As if his last escape route was closing inexorably.

He did not give up easily. He phoned Miriam the next day, and the day after that, and each day for the week following. Each time her maid said, 'Who is calling?' Then, 'Miss Crenshaw does not care to speak to you.'

Slade wrote her a letter, in which he said, 'After all I can have the eye covered with grafted skin.' He followed up the letter with a personal visit. But Miriam was 'out.'

It was fairly ultimate. Particularly when a detective called the next day, and asked him to cease his 'persecution' of his former wife. The officer was considerably impressed by the beautiful residence, but he was a man who knew his duty. 'We have received a complaint, y'understand. We'll have to take action if it continues, y'understand?'

Slade understood. His little dream was over.

STATEMENT MADE TO
CORONER'S JURY BY
WILFRED STANTON

I was first employed by Michael Slade as a houseman about five years ago. I was with him, with only a brief holiday, throughout the past year.

My employer was away from home several times during that period. He always seemed in an upset condition after each such absence, but he did not take me into his confidence. Before his final departure, I noticed a new air of decisiveness about him, as if he had finally made up his mind about something after a long uncertainty. He bought a second automatic, a match to the one he already had, and a great deal of ammunition for both weapons. He also purchased other items, but I did not see what was in the packages that arrived for him. He read almost continuously. I remember one book dealt with metallurgy, another was a volume on physics, and a third about the new rocket ships.

All this time, too, he was sitting out in the yard with his eye charts. These exercises were unusual in that he wore a light durable hunting suit made of waterproof materials, which he had had made. In addition he carried two automatics, a hunting knife and a pouch of ammunition. His pockets also seemed to be stuffed, but I don't know what was in them.

Mr. Slade was aware of my awareness of the unusualness of this get-up, and he seemed amused at my anxiety. One day, he told me not to be alarmed if he went away without warning.

It was the day after that that I called him for lunch, and he was gone. His disappearance was unusual in that the chair and the charts were just as he had left them, and particularly unusual in that there was snow on the ground, and his tracks should have been visible leading out of the yard. I saw no tracks that would indicate a departure.

I can only say that I was surprised when Mr. Slade's dead body was discovered last week two hundred miles from here. He was obviously expecting something to happen. And it did.

CHAPTER SIX

The change this time was like the click of a camera shutter. He felt his eyes working, then his house vanished, and then –

It was raining, a warm but heavy rain. The water came down on the marsh near the caves in a multitude of slanting drops, like millions of tiny knives cutting the surface. Under that blurring curtain of water, the landscape looked wilder, less civilised. Its very green lusciousness made it primitive, but the green was there, ornamental and gorgeous.

Slade, who had started to mull over the problem of rain in one plane of existence and snow in another, under the same sun, felt a warm, wet trickle of water run down inside the collar of his waterproof suit. It didn't bother him, but it took his mind off of the why of the rain. He stepped automatically under the overhanging branch of a nearby tree, and from its uncertain shelter – the water poured from it – peered up at the ledge.

Some of the excitement died out of him. The hill looked lifeless. All the fires were out, and not a human being was in sight. It was the rain, of course. They'd be inside the caves.

Since he had no intention of climbing to the ledge until he had been discovered – spears and knives might flash just a little too swiftly if he surprised them in their caves – his problem was to find shelter. He constructed himself a crude house of dead branches overlaid with large, fronded leaves. Then he scraped away a heavy layer of wet leaves, and was pleasantly surprised to find that the ground underneath was comparatively dry.

He slept fitfully throughout the afternoon and evening. During the night he was awake for a long time. Just before he finally slept, he thought sharply, 'I'll have to wake up before they do.'

When he opened his eyes, the sun was shining from a blue sky. And several three-eyed men were kneeling around the open end of his shelter. Beyond them were other men, and in the farther background, women and children.

Very slowly, Slade sat up. He pushed the shelter over on its side, and climbed to his feet, but that too, was an automatic movement. The convulsive thought came that the strain inside his head and in his muscles would produce organic tensions strong enough to precipitate him back to the United States.

But nothing happened. The people and the marsh and the cave hill remained in his vision as steady as sanity itself. He was welded to this plane of existence as if he had been born here.

It was not until that thought had come and gone that he noticed none of the men carried arms of any descripion. The relief that came was almost as tremendous as had been the first shock. Before he could speak, one of the men nearest him said gently :

'Careful. You're not completely stable yet.'

The man reached forward and placed his palm over Slade's centre eye. The movement was too unexpected for it to be resisted. The delayed reaction, when it finally came, was half-hearted. Slade started to take a step backwards, and then, realising the meaning of what was happening, he stopped in amazement.

These people knew that he was not of this plane. *And they knew why.* The next thought followed hard on the first :

The cave dwellers were NOT primitives.

It was too big an idea to grasp all in one instant, particularly as the man who had touched his forehead now stepped back with a smile, and said :

'I think you will be all right.'

Slade hadn't noticed the fellow's voice before. Now, he did. It was calm and melodic, without harshness, the words so easily spoken that they were like a flow of music produced by a master.

That fact, also, held his mind only a moment. He stood looking around him at the men and at the women, and his relief grew second by second. They were smiling, friendly; they were good-looking and alert, a high physical and mental type. Slade allowed himself a flashing memory of the degenerate blood addicts of the city of Naze, and comprehend with finality that, whatever was the basic reason for the deadly siege of the city by the ship of Leear, these clean and decent-looking cave dwellers were evidence in favour of the ship.

He realised that it was time he said something. He said, 'Thank you. I am a friend. My name is Michael Slade.'

The tall, eagle-eyed man who had already spoken nodded. 'My name,' he said, 'is Danbar.'

They shook hands. It was so simply, so generously done that Slade was not sure then or ever afterwards as to whether shaking hands was a common custom among these people. Or whether Danbar had instantaneously and without hesitation responded to the habits of a stranger.

As their hands separated, Slade noted for the first time that the man was inches taller than himself, and marvelously strong-looking. He had a lean, handsome face. Except for his extra eye, he would have been good-looking in any group of two-eyed human beings. He seemed about thirty years old.

He smiled. He took Slade's arm, and led him to another man, a splendid-looking chap who had been watching the proceedings from the background.

Danbar indicated the other, 'Malenkens,' he said.

The way he said it made it sound a distinctive and important name. And, looking at the man, Slade did not doubt but that he was being introduced to one of the leaders of the tribe. With Malenkens, too, the handshake was warm, but the smile was sterner, more aloof.

Danbar said, 'You can meet the others later. Now, let us return to the ledge for breakfast.'

Contact was established as easy as that.

The winding path that led up to the caves was made of cement steps flanked by ornamental shrubs. A cement sidewalk ran along the entire length of the ledge, with smaller sidewalks leading into the caves. In between the sidewalks, green velvety grass grew in neat plots that could only have been planned by skilful gardeners.

Slade, pausing before the first cave, peered into an interior at least as uncavelike as what he had already seen. The floor was of cement, but it was covered with throw rugs. The walls and ceiling were plastered over a base of cement. The chairs, tables and bunks that he could see were of unpainted wood, but they were well designed and had been sandpapered to a smooth polish. The overall result was astonishingly modern.

Danbar touched Slade's arm, and mentioned him to follow Malenkens, who was proceeding along the ledge. As he walked, Slade found himself surreptitiously looking for Leear. He was not greatly surprised when he failed to locate her, but neither did he accept her absence as final. She had been here once. There was no reason why she should not come back. And, besides, she must know that this would be his point of entry into the three-eyed world.

Malenkens stopped, and spoke for the first time. 'In here,' he said.

The cave was a structural duplicate of the one into which Slade had peered. The three men sat down in chairs, and Malenkens spoke again.

'Slade,' he said, 'we have been estimating your situation from the time you wakened, and in my judgement it will take about six years to adjust the rhythm of your life to our group. That takes into account your untrained resistance, and the fact that it will probably require several months for you to help Leear destroy the barrier of Naze and Geean. And of course, it assumes that you will not be killed or dangerously injured.'

He added, 'I am not trying to alarm you. I am merely stating the facts as I see them. Now, Danbar will take over.'

Danbar did not move, but continued to sit in his chair. He looked at Slade speculatively. 'You will be wondering,' he said, 'what Malenkens was talking about. Watch.'

He vanished.

For a minute, Slade sat where he was. He had no particular thoughts, though the memory came that, when Leear had hovered above him near the granary, he had not been able to see her against the stars. She, too, must have been invisible.

At the end of the minute, it struck him perhaps he was expected to do something. He stood up, bent over Danbar's chair, and gingerly moved his arm through the space where Danbar had been sitting. There was no resistance to the movement. He glanced over at Malenkens, but the man did not look up.

Slade sat down again, heavily this time, trembling a little. There was no reason at all why Danbar, having rendered himself invisible, had not climbed to his feet and walked in a leisurely fashion to the cave entrance, or perhaps he was standing beside his chair, watching his guest's reaction. There was no reason why he shouldn't have done one of those things, but Slade had the vaguely sinking conviction that Danbar had done nothing of the kind, and that in fact he was still sitting in the chair.

Primitives, Slade thought. *And I believe they were primitives.*

132

These people had learned the innermost secrets of the human nervous system. They were so far ahead of their two-eyed cousins that comparison seemed almost ridiculous. Or wait a minute – what was it Malenkens had said? '. . . *It will take you about six years to adjust the rhythm of your life to our group –*'

The first burning excitement stirred Slade. Did he mean that at the end of six years, he too, might be able to render himself invisible at will? Or did he mean – ?

Slade pressed the thought back into his mind. He forced himself to lean back in his chair. He parted his lips to speak to Malenkens, then closed them again. The man was looking the other way. The moments dragged, and there was no sign of Danbar. His absence began to be disturbing. For the second time the possibility occurred to Slade that he was expected to do something.

He stood up uncertainly. On a sudden impulse he seated himself in Danbar's chair. That didn't last long. The thought came that it would be a very humourless situation if the man chose to materialise in the chair.

Slade walked to the entrance of the cave on the doubtful expectation that Danbar would be outside. The ledge was a veritable hive of activity, fires burning brightly, women stirring caldrons, children already becoming nuisances with their games and noise. But of Danbar there was no sign.

Slade stood for a moment peering out over the marsh. The view was gorgeous beyond all imagination. The water gleamed in the sun, and it was alive with colourful growth. Far out, he caught a glimpse of birds fluttering, and he thought with a thrill: Three-eyed birds! In the distance beyond the marsh trees reared to amazing heights, and he could see the haze of mounting hills beyond. Everywhere was the green of perpetual summer.

Slade turned back into the cavern, quivering inside. What a wonderful plane of Earth he was on. Never, surely, would he have the slightest desire to return whence he had come.

There was, of course, the problem of Naze – That brought Slade back to reality with a start. He saw that Danbar had still not rematerialised. He thought, 'Invisibility? If I had to figure out some way of making myself invisible, knowing what I do now about the art of seeing, I would try to disturb in some way the vision centers of those who were looking at me. Perfect vision is possible only when the mind is relaxed. Therefore I would try to tense their minds in some way.'

The rationalisation brought a sudden startled thought. Why, of course. He *was* expected to do something. He drew a deep, slow breath, and let it out with a sighing sound, simultaneously letting all his muscles go lax. The eye specialist, Dr. McIver, had always maintained that the human body could relax with one breath.

In that instant Slade proved it. As he started to draw his second breath, Danbar reappeared in his chair. The man looked up earnestly at Slade.

'Very good, my friend. I was hoping that you would manage to figure that out for yourself.' He went on, 'You have experienced for yourself one of the basic truths of the human nervous system. During the next few months you will be taught the ultimate secrets of relaxation, relaxation so complete that, even in the final issue, there is no limit to the control that can be exercised over it. But now –'

He stood up, smiling. 'Let us,' he said, 'take our chairs outside and have breakfast.'

Slade followed the two men out into the brilliant sun.

CHAPTER SEVEN

On the thirty-second day of his stay with the tribe, Slade lay at ease on a knoll above the marsh. From his position, he could see the caves about a mile away. It was a marvelous day. It had rained a little in the morning, but now the sky was as clear and blue as could be. Before him, in a garden-like vista, the green, green grass and shrubbery still sparkled with raindrops that hung heavy on every blade and sprig and leaf and branch.

The whole world around him was as wonderful as ever, and yet Slade was conscious of dissatisfaction. 'I'm an active person,' he thought. 'My nerves are still afflicted with the neurotic desire to do things.'

He even had an impulse pushing at him. That odd metal device that he had found half-buried in the ground near his farm the night he had seen Leear in a shadowed corridor of an old spaceship – it would be interesting to go and get it, and examine it.

He did not move. He had to admit that the previous month had, in its way, been exciting. The world of relaxation was an inward world of unending discovery. His knowledge began with the muscles, lectures about and exercises with. Exercises? It was not exactly the right word for what he was doing. Slade had decided, but he continued to use it for want of a better. Exercise suggested physical activity, but the relaxation exercises were the reverse of movement. They were stillness. They were inhalation and exhalation as effortlessly as possible. They were long minutes of lying upon carefully arranged pillows while the mind concentrated gently upon certain muscles, and always the message his brain sent was: 'Let go, let go, let go.'

Gradually, over the weeks, he learned the basic philosophy behind the relaxation. A correct posture, and good breathing habits. When at fault, those two things alone caused tension repercussions that affected the entire body. Tension made for bad vision and poor hearing. Tension was responsible for quick fatigue, for lack of strength and for narcotic cravings. Tension caused the kidneys to inject a fluid into the blood which caused high blood pressure, melancholy and a negative attitude towards life. Tension subtly changed the acid content of the digestive fluids. Tension was literally, the devil of the nervous system, but getting rid of it was merely the first, preliminary step to the control of the body.

The second phase was normalisation of the nerves. Every nerve, individually and collectively, was capable of a positive or negative action. It could pass an impulse to seek another path to the brain. It was doubtful if more than five percent of an ordinary person's nerve impulses followed direct routes. It was true, of course, that many of the detours were used over and over again, but it was no justification for a bad habit to point out that it was repeated endlessly, particularly when the cumulative results were *un*sanity, early old age and a confused mind.

The entire ninety-five percent of misdirected nervous energy had to be re-channeled along direct routes and this was done by concentrating on key nerve paths. In every case, positive training was necessary. As with muscular relaxation, one could not just seek out a lazy environment and take it easy. Definite things had to be done. Muscles consistently relaxed by a system eventually stayed relaxed. Nerves repeatedly told to establish a direct channel, with a picture of that channel clearly visualised, did eventually make the exact channel demanded.

Nerve control led to the third or molecular phase, about which, when Slade asked him, Danbar merely said, 'You will see. You will see.'

Lying there on the knoll above the marsh, it seemed to Slade that he knew the muscular relaxation exercises sufficiently well to be able to do them for a short time without an instructor standing by. He should be able to walk to the area where his farm existed on the Earth plane, and get the machine buried in the ground there.

He climbed to his feet with sudden decision. *I'll ask Danbar or Malenkens*, he thought.

Danbar, to whom Slade made the request, after the evening exercises, looked disturbed. Then he glanced questioningly at Malenkens. It was the latter who said:

'Leear told us you would be restless.' He paused, frowning. Then he looked at Slade from under lowered lashes. 'I've decided to be fairly frank with you, Slade. We are training you to help Leear against Naze. You must not think that we are parties to her plan. We merely exercise certain restraints upon her. You may wonder what that means, so I will explain.

'It is Leear's intention,' he went on, 'to involve you again in Naze. We have no power to prevent her from doing that, nor actually do we want to. Somehow, Geean must be killed, and the people of Naze freed. According to Leear, only you can do this, how she has never explained.

'What we did was to delay her plans until you could be given at least preliminary training in our marvelous system.'

He finished quietly, 'I think you will agree that, under these circumstances, you would be wise not to involve yourself in minor side issues.'

Slade was shocked. The more he thought about it the greater grew his shock. It was curious but, though he had not for a minute forgotten Leear or Naze – incredible Naze – somehow the long sweet month of pastoral existence had blurred the darker potentialities of that memory.

Now, here it was, plainly stated. On occasion in his past life, he had a reputation for facing facts with a brutal honesty, and his comparisons had startled his business associates. That was the way he finally looked at his present position. The comparison that occurred to him was that he was like a pig being fattened for the slaughter.

He spent the night, narrow-eyed, sleeping fitfully, and in a fury every time he woke up. By morning his mind was made up.

So Malenkens and the others had only persuaded Leear with difficulty to delay putting him immediately in jeopardy. Well, that was just fine. He owed her nothing anyway but a punch in the nose for being indirectly responsible for the death of Amor and Caldra.

Since her intention was to use him without so much as a by your leave, his purpose could only be to prevent her by every possible means from involving him.

The determination gave him considerable satisfaction until near morning, when it occurred to him that it might not be any too easy to prevent her machinations. The trouble was he knew so little, so desperately little. He had not the faintest idea what methods might be available to these people who knew the innermost secrets of the human nervous system, and in addition had a spaceship loaded with gadgets, one at least of which was capable of transmitting material objects from this plane of the Earth plane and back again.

The new possibilities calmed him. He would have to be very clever indeed, to ensure that she didn't get him into Naze again. And anger would be his poorest asset in carrying out that purpose.

At breakfast time, he emerged from his cave, seated himself beside Malenkens, and said :

'I think it's time that I find out something about the history behind the war beween the ship and the city.'

Malenkens said, 'I see that you have been thinking of what I told you last night.' Slade waited, and Malenkens went on, 'I do not regret having said it, but I cannot say more. We promised Leear that we would let her tell you the entire story.'

'Then tell me,' said Slade savagely, 'who is Leear?'

'She is one of the silver belts.'

'One of the what?'

Malenkens was grave. 'Her personal plans for you would suffer a psychological defeat if I told you more. You must wait. I can say this. If you survive the destruction of Naze, the universe will be yours for the taking.'

Temporarily that silenced Slade. Coming from Malenkens, those were momentous words. They brought his first sense of exhilaration at the greatness of the adventure into which his destiny had brought him.

The exhilaration was brief. The tremendousness of the reward implied by Malenkens suggested an enormous compensating sacrifice. Slade stiffened slowly. He disliked the thought of being on an unfriendly basis with these kindly people, but it was time he stated his position without equivocation.

He did so, pretty much as he had already decided. No co-operation with Leear until he was good and ready. It was ridiculous for her to assume that a man could be shoved blindly into a situation, again and again, and told to get out as best he could, each time without having more than a sketchy idea as to what was going on. He for one refused to have anything to do with such a plan. And if he ever went in, it would be on the basis of full information with his eyes wide open.

'You will have to kill a man,' said Malenkens in a strangely drab voice. 'You have never killed a human being. It is Leear's unalterable conviction that you could not bring yourself to commit a cold-blooded murder, and that only under the stress of violent danger could you be nerved to kill. Such is her opinion, and, having observed you for an entire moon period, I agree with her.'

'Thanks,' said Slade dryly. 'I'm still not interested.'

He finished his meal in silence. He felt uncertain as to just what his position was with the tribe, but he decided in the end that what had happened was not a breakup. He would remain for a while at least, and make his plans on the basis of careful thought. There was no use rushing off, half cocked.

He attended his morning relaxation exercises as usual.

During the second month, the tempo of his life seemed faster to Slade. He realised what it was. He was more alert, more wary, eager to learn things. He kept a watchful eye on the men, and slept with a gun under his pillow.

Towards the end of the month, it struck him that no one in the tribe had ever seen the automatics in action. And that it might be a good idea to fire one of his precious bullets as a sort of a deterrent. He hesitated about that, because even one bullet might be important in a crisis. And yet, it seemed clear that Leear would never get him into Naze against his will unless male members of the tribe trussed him up; and gave him into her power.

It was a month of several discoveries. He had been wondering about the animal life of this plane, 'It's there,' Malenkens assured him, with an odd smile. 'It all depends on whether they decide to find out your reaction to seeing them.'

That didn't quite make sense, but over a period of four weeks he had glimpses. And, finally, every time, the glimpse revealed the animal watching *him*. There was a tiny, dark creature too fast for a clear picture to form of its shape. A long, slim, spotted beast, too thin to be well muscled, and resembling a dog, trotted off disdainfully into the brush, after looking Slade over with an aloof eye. There was a horselike beast that peered at him though for several seconds, and then galloped off snorting. And then, finally, there was a really shocking meeting with an animal.

Slade was walking along in a pathless valley adjoining the valley of the caves when a chance glance to the rear revealed a beast bigger than himself trotting along not more than ten yards behind him. It had a head that had both cat and bear features, and its body was long, and sleek and greyish-brown.

It was the same type of beast that had bent over him that night in Caldra's and Amor's apartment.

Slade felt a thrill as sharp as fear, and snatched at his automatic. The animal's teeth glinted like knives as it snarled at him. Its great paws came up. It whirled, and dived into concealing brush.

A nith, Danbar told him, and then was silent when Slade described what had happened in the apartment in Naze. Later, Slade saw him talking earnestly to Malenkens. The two men fell silent as Slade approached, so he was pretty certain they had been talking about him.

It was startling, that sudden discovery that he was being discussed. It emphasised the unsatisfactoriness of his position, and made immediately necessary, it seemed to Slade, a demonstration of his powerful weapons.

He had been thinking about the best method for doing that, and finally it seemed to him that he had it. A bird. For two months he had watched birds with gay plumage frisking through the foliage over and around the marsh. Wary were those birds. He could spend an hour crawling towards a flock. And then, just before he got close enough for a good look, the birds would take off towards a remote destination. Gradually, his desire to have a close look at a winged creature with three eyes became almost an obsession.

It seemed to him, now that if he could shoot one from the ledge, he would, figuratively, kill two birds with one stone.

On the following morning, he brought a chair out of his cave, laid one of his automatics on his lap, and sat watching the brush below. After ten minutes, he noted that people were glancing at him from the corner of their eyes. A few minutes after that, Danbar pulled up a chair and sat down beside him.

'What makes you think,' he asked, 'that your weapon will fire in this plane of existence?'

'Eh!' said Slade.

After a moment, the possibilities stunned him. He took careful aim at a distant flock of birds. He paused to say, 'This gun makes a loud noise, so prepare yourself.' Then he squeezed the trigger.

Click!

It was an empty sound. It left Slade with the chilled feeling that he was naked and helpless. The sun was as warm as ever, but for two months his two automatics had given him confidence and courage. They buttressed his spirit every time he thought of how easily the several dozen tribesmen could overpower him and give him to Leear.

Now, that buttress was gone.

For a moment, Slade sat quite still, then he ejected the cartridge into his palm, and began to pry out the bullet. He spilled the powder onto the cement sidewalk in a little pile, and then walked over to the nearest fire and picked up a burning faggot. He touched the flame to the powder. It burned with a slow sputter, like thick paper. Beside him Danbar said:

'The chemical combination will have to be slightly different. I have no doubt it could be made to work.'

Slade had no intention of waiting to find out. His protection was gone. Without a word, he entered his cave, strapped on his second automatic, stuffed into his pockets the smaller articles he had brought from Earth – and returned to the outside. Danbar fell into step beside him.

'You are leaving us, Slade?'

Slade said, 'Where is Malenkens?'

'He's gone.'

That was the second great shock. 'Gone! Where to?'

He saw that Danbar was looking at him oddly. 'Malenkens is not one of us, Slade. He visits us occasionally. He is one of the . . . silver belts.'

Slade was silent. He realised what had happened. He had been handed over to one of the Leear hierarchy. For the first time it struck him how consistently Malenkens had been in the foreground of his tribal life. Danbar was speaking again:

'Do not blame us too severely, Slade, for anything that happens. None of us here have attained further than the molecular phase of body control. We are helpless in this struggle between the ship and the city, and so long as the city exists we can never attain the final stage of self-control.

'It is a jarring factor. Its existence prevents certain basic rhythms. The *thought* that people like ourselves are caught behind its barrier, forever unable to escape – and that is the main purpose of the barrier – to keep those people there under Geean's control – weighs upon our spirit, and makes it impossible for us to realise our potentialities. And the result of that is that we, too, are at the mercy of Geean.'

Slade had the impression that he was listening to an apology. It thawed him. 'Thank you,' he said, 'I have nothing but friendship for your people here.'

Danbar said, 'Go with luck, my friend.'

It took more than an hour before the cave ledge was finally out of sight.

CHAPTER EIGHT

The scene grew wilder by the hour. He saw no animals, but birds by the hundreds squawked in the brush and in the trees, on average a very different type of bird than those that had been in the vicinity of the caves. They were less wary. Frequently, he could walk right past them without disturbing them. Towards evening, he picked up a stick and knocked two pigeonlike creatures out of a low shrub, and had his first three-eyed birds.

In that dusk, with his fire sputtering defiance at the gathering darkness, with the cries of the night birds all around, he ate fresh fruit and pigeon roasted over a spit.

After eating, Slade pondered the problem of two-eyed and three-eyed creatures, and the worlds they lived in. There must be common ancestry. The human form would not have repeated easily. Way back, various creatures of the two-eyed world had developed a third eye, and had one automatically, without their even being aware of it, into this special universe.

Actually, like sight and sense itself, the explanation probably went to the very roots of reality. What didn't exist for the mind, the senses ignored. And in some intricate fashion, the object or objects ceased to affect the body as a whole.

It was not a new idea. But the old formulation expressed by the phrase, 'Is the cat sleeping under the stove while I'm not around?' failed to take into account the certainties of the human mind. The absolute conviction that the cat was there whether the observer was present or not. Blind folk acquired certainties from hearing and touch.

The mind alone counted.

As the night wore on, Slade began to think, in the uneasy periods between dozes, of guns that wouldn't shoot. It was a thought that was to occur again and again during the days that followed. It almost but not quite altered his plans.

He had intended to get the metal device, then turn sharply southward, and so walk entirely out of the territory of Naze and Leear. It was an unheroic role that he proposed for himself and it made him a little defensive, a little ashamed.

Here am I, he thought, in the strangest adventure a man ever got into, and I'm playing it cautious.

There were men, he knew, who would not hesitate a minute about plunging deep into the affair. Such men would now be on their way to Naze with the intention of bearding Geean in his great central tower.

Lying in the darkness, Slade's lips tightened. It was no use kidding himself. Not for him was the bold course. The important thing was that he do not let caution send him southward without the metal object. It might prove without value. But it was a clue, and who could tell, it *might* still be in a workable condition. He couldn't leave it behind him.

The forests were quiet, the valleys long, the hills gradually higher. A great, virgin continent spread before his footsteps, but the amazing realisation was the sensational familiarity of the route. There was a slight difference in the depth of the canyons and the height of the hills. The extensive marshes, the trees and the forests of shrubs were absolutely different. But the general contours were the same. And he had made the hundred mile trip to his farm so often that he wasn't lost for a minute. It was a wonderful feeling.

He came finally on the sixth morning to the long, hilly plain at the end of which – on the Earth plane – was his farm. Very cautiously, using every possible cover, he approached the point where the spaceship had been that night. From afar, he saw that it was not there, but his caution did not relax for a minute.

Within ten minutes of reaching the area, he found the machine. He used a sturdy branch he had picked up en route as a crowbar to pry it out of the ground. It was deeply imbedded, and it took considerable perspiration and twenty minutes to loosen it.

It came up finally, and showed its shape. A boxlike affair, with a wheel attached to one end. It was not too small in size, but its lightness was amazing. Pure magnesium, or even lithium, might have matched it, but little else.

He estimated the weight of the box and the wheel together at something less than thirty pounds. It glittered in the sun, untarnished by its long exposure. Slade made no effort to examine it immediately.

All that day, he carried it on first one shoulder, then another. About an hour before dusk he came to a burbling creek, and decided to stay there for the night. It was rather exposed, but he was tired, and the nearest forest looked many miles away.

He ate hurriedly, then, his curiosity as strong as ever, he bent over the machine. Atomic and magnetic power, Malenkens had told him once, were the energy sources of old Naze. 'Naturally,' the man had pointed out, 'they will work a little differently here than where you came from.'

After his experience with his automatics, Slade could appreciate that. Nevertheless, he decided that he preferred this one to be magnetic.

He studied the machine intently.

It was the wheel that puzzled him. Only one wheel. And so large, too. The metal box, into which the shaft of the wheel disappeared, was only about a foot cube. The wheel was a little over two feet in diameter, and it curved out from the shaft like a flower with long petals that formed a cup shape. It was big enough to be a small cornucopia. It could have acted easily as a small mixer, so spacious was it.

'Hm-m-m!' said Slade.

Perhaps the angle was not to think of it as a wheel just because it rotated easily on a shaft.

Still, it looked like a wheel.

He spun it. It whirled and finally came to a stop. Nothing else happened.

He fumbled over the box, searching for a control device. In a way he had done that before. Now, however, he was thorough. But there was nothing.

He noticed three brighter spots on one shiny side of the machine. They looked like dents made in the hard substance. But there were no dents. His probing fingers sensed not the slightest depression.

Puzzled, Slade examined the brightnesses. He brought them close to his eyes. Glitter, glitter, he thought. Wonder what –

Something caught at his eyes.

He jerked back, letting the machine drop.

It didn't drop. It hung a foot from his face, the wheel facing up, the three bright spots like tiny blazing fires poking at his three eyes.

He closed them, then blinked rapidly. The blaze points pierced through his eyelids. In a panic, Slade shoved at the box.

The machine glided a hundred feet through the air, and came to a stop. The three bright spots poured fire towards his eyes, as bright as if he was still a foot away. The extra distance made no difference.

Slade raced towards the machine. Have to turn it away from him, or the thing would destroy his vision. He caught it with trembling hands. And turned it upside down.

It spun around without resistance. And its mind-frightening connection with his eyes broken, it wafted gently, almost balloonlike, to the ground. Slade hid it in the brush beside the creek. Then, still shaking from his experience, lay down on the grassy bank. It was only slowly that he realised that nothing damaging had happened. His vision was as good as ever. His eyes felt cool and rested, and quite untensed.

He slept dreamlessly and without wakening all night. When he opened his eyes, the sun was just coming up. He busied himself gathering fruit from nearby trees, and he had just finished eating when a thin whistling sound rent the air to one side of him.

Slade jumped a foot as something struck the grass where he had been.

CHAPTER NINE

He whirled, and stared at the object. A noose made of metal looking rope. It was alive in a mechanical fashion. It shuddered and narrowed, tightening as he watched it. Its two ends withdrew into a little metal box.

Before Slade could examine it further, there was another hissing sound. The second noose struck his shoulder, as he twisted aside. It bounded away like a rubber ball, almost hitting a nearby tree.

'What the –' said Slade. And dived behind a shrub. By the time he reached it, two more nooses were lying on the grass, writhing shut. Slade slid his gaze around the horizon – and saw their source.

Flying things! They were too far away to be clearly visible. They seemed to have legs but no wings. He caught a glint of scarlet, then dazzling silver, then green, and of human-like arms clinging to somehing that shimmered above them. It was the shimmering objects that flew. The creatures merely hung on.

And every little while, though the motion that caused it was lost in the distance, one of the creatures would send a noose hissing towards Slade's head.

He felt a horrid thrill. What was this? With an absolutely gruesome fascination, he remembered the girl's letter. Geean and the hunters of the city.

But the hunters were keeping their distance.

A thousand yards, he estimated shakily. Even if they had worked, his automatics would have been useless at that distance. He looked around frantically for a way of escape. But the nearest forest was about ten miles behind him. There was brush, there were shrubs, and by heaven, there was no reason to lose hope until he was actually caught.

Five nooses sprang around him while he observed and had the thought. He began to gather them up frantically. They were probably accustomed to retrieving them, and they couldn't have too many.

He darted behind a shrub. From its shelter he flicked his gaze calculatingly towards every horizon, counting he creatures. One, two . . . seven.

Slade thought jerkily, 'If I can keep them off till dark.'

A glance towards the sun showed that it hadn't moved a fraction of an inch, seemingly, from its position low above the eastern horizon.

Night was a long, long way off.

His lips tightened. Some of the fever went out of him. His body grew calm with determination. Straight ahead. There was no reason why, with a show of bravado, he shouldn't be able to make it – straight ahead to that distant forest.

As he twisted towards a second shrub, a noose came down from the sky, ringed him, spun a little as it struck his shoulders. And then settled down over his arms, tightening with irresistible strength.

Slade grabbed for his sheathed knife. But his hands were pressed too tightly against his body. He jerked at the snare, and stumbled over a stone, fell hard, rolling over and over.

The noose was like a steel spring. It cut into his flesh with a strength that made Slade gasp. There must be a releasing catch – Have to release it.

He strained to get his fingers up to it, but its hold was too cunning for him. As he struggled, Slade caught a movement in the near sky. It was hard to see through the pain tears that had started into his eyes. But he blinked the tears aside, and, after a moment, he saw the silver-clad hunters clearly. They were about a hundred feet away, and swooping closer.

He ceased his hopeless fight.

The seven hunters of the city dropped from their flying devices twenty feet away. Slade looked them over briefly, wondering if Geean was among them. It seemed unlikely. Swiftly, he forgot the men. It was the reddish flying instruments that snatched all his attention. They clung for a minute to the air above the men. And then, like slowly deflating balloons, they collapsed to the ground. One man carried a spare flyer.

Each instrument was a red-frosted, glasslike extrusion about three inches in diameter and three feet long. There was a sling attached to it, and at the end of the sling some handgrips.

Nothing else. No machinery, no apparent source of energy – Slade had an impulse to make it a closer examination. He repressed it, partly because the noose held him as tightly as

148

ever. And partly because he had his first *close* look at the men.

The day he had seen the soldiers of Geean in Caldra's and Amor's apartment, he hadn't really had time to note character. Now, with these henchmen, he did.

They were intent faces, dissipated looking, very light in colour. They bent over him, and two of them were smiling sardonically. One of the men said something, and there was a quick general laughter, that ended, and left the faces intent again. Slade didn't catch the words.

Slade felt the automatics taken from the holsters, and other articles removed from his pockets. Each item was swiftly scanned, then stuffed into a canvaslike bag. Before the search was finished, one of the men fumbled at the noose. It loosened promptly, and came up easily over his head.

And, again, there was speed. Even as Slade climbed to his feet and started to rub the numbness out of his arms, another man shoved the handgrips of the spare flier into his fingers, and pointed at a third, who was just picking one of the fliers off the ground.

'Watch him,' he said curtly.

As Slade watched, the third man swung the bar up in front of him with an easy rhythmic swing. And, simultaneously, with dexterity, leaped into the air.

The glasslike bar caught at something. It stiffened, straightened, and pointed like an arrow from a bow. It began to glide forward with the man clinging to the handgrips – as the man beside Slade said curtly, 'Now, you.'

He expected the thing to come crashing down on his head. And, simultaneously, paradoxically, he expected his arms would be half torn out of their sockets when the device caught 'onto' the air.

But it wasn't like that. It wasn't like that at all. It didn't fall. There was no tug, no jerk. Something, a current, a – lightness – saturated his body. And it was that current, and not the machine, that lifted him. Lifted him like thistledown borne on a climbing breeze.

Strong as metal, the flying device rode above him. But it was only a catalytic agent, *affecting* his body not transporting it. His body flew with the machine, was of the machine. The two became one. He remembered how the bars had dropped a few minutes before, after the hunters let go, and it was clear that neither could remain airborne without the other.

A great basic force welded a union between his nervous system and the machine. And the dead weight of gravity let go of him. It was like the wheel machine, he recalled with a start. He glanced back towards where he had hidden the machine, but it was not visible from the air.

The relief that came had mixed in it great wonder. What incredible secrets of the nervous system had these people discovered, both natural and mechanical? He saw that the other six hunters were swooping up to him. They clustered around him, clinging to their fliers effortlessly. And somehow the sweep of their machines became the direction and speed of his. It was as if his flier was guided by a sympathetic union with the other machines.

They soared low over the land and over a whole series of marshes, in and out along valleys and through forests. Slade noticed that the fliers had a tendency to remain near the ground. Not once was there a real attempt to climb high. They went around and between trees, not over them. They avoided the towering, snow-capped mountains that flanked their course. Like a river, they flowed along the easiest course, and in the end he decided that the motive power was derived from the magnetic currents of Earth. Nothing else, in view of what he knew, could explain the evenness of their course, and the *type* of transportation.

In a surprisingly short time, the clustered group of them came within sight of a city of shining spires. Slade stared at it with glistening eyes because it was one thing to have seen it from inside, quite another to view it like this. It was about four miles wide at the mouth of a widening valley. He couldn't see how long it was. The fliers were too low, and the city stood on a plateau.

Its towers and roofs glinted in the brilliant rising sun. Clearly now, its design was apparent. The whole city sloped up towards the central tower of Geean, that reared like a pylon into the lower heavens. The height of that pylon seemed greater than he remembered it. It rivaled the near mountain peaks, and from its silvery eminence, a hazy, violet glow spread like a mist covering the whole city. The colour was remarkably sharp seen from this angle. It was a mist of light that curved like a carefully worn robe onto the grass a mile from every outskirt of the city.

The fliers poised before the barrier. For a moment only. A signal flashed mirror-bright from the distant tower, and the red-frosted devices flowed forward and through the barrier like so many knives cutting through thin gauze.

They almost grazed the rooftops of low built homes. They evaded several spires, and then began to swoop lower. They were twenty feet, then ten feet from the ground. A man reached over and grasped one handle of Slade's machine.

'Let go,' he said curtly. 'Drop.'

Slade looked at him, amazed and uncomprehending. The surly face, so close to his own was venomous.

'Drop!'

Slade glanced down. A cobbled street was below. He hesitated, then let go. The instant return of weight made a thrill in his nervous system. He struck the ground harder than he liked. Twice, he rolled over, and then he was up. The fliers were already disappearing around a nearby spire.

Abruptly, he was alone.

STATEMENT TO THE CORONER'S JURY
By John Alden, Farmer,
Smailes County

It is my custom to arise at 5 a.m. every morning. On the morning of the 19th I got up at my usual hour, and I was doing my chores when I observed what seemed to me a strange spectacle.

A woman and a large bearlike beast were walking in a westerly direction across my stubble field. Since bears are frequently dangerous, the fear came to me that the woman did not know she was being followed by so large and formidable an animal.

I ran and procured my gun, but though I was inside only a minute, and there was no place where anybody could have gone to in such a short time, when I came out of the house, there was no sign of either woman or beast. Almost literally they disappeared into thin air.

It was a little after noon that same day that the smashed body of Michael Slade was discovered in the high valley two miles from my place. According to the doctor, he had died about half an hour before he was found. So it is very likely his death had no connection with the woman and the bear, whom I saw earlier.

But I report the incident for what it is worth in clearing up the mystery of the three-eyed man.

Except for the foregoing, I had never seen Michael Slade until his dead body was brought to my farm by the doctor.

One more thing: When the police from Smailes County and I examined the tracks of the woman and the animal, we discovered that they ended abruptly in the middle of the field.

I am not prepared to offer an explanation for this.

CHAPTER TEN

Slade walked slowly along, examining his position. His automatics were gone, but his knife was still in its holster. His handkerchief had been left in his pocket as well as a small case of fishing tackle and a box of morphine tablets, which he had brought along in the event of a violent accident befalling him.

Abruptly, he discovered that the side street he was on was not quite so deserted as it had first appeared. An old woman sidled hurriedly out of an alleyway, and muttered:

'Blood! or I'll murder you tonight.' Slade brushed her aside, thinking: *Why had they released him? What did they expect him to do? Do! That was it of course. Geean thought he knew about the plotting that was going on, and somehow the great man of Naze expected him to lead his forces to the plotters.*

Slade laughed grimly. There was a great deal of cunning common sense in Geean's plan, but it had a basic fault. Geean was wrong in his belief that Slade knew anything.

But that didn't matter now. His purpose before the fall of night must be to find the apartment that had once been occupied by Caldra and Amor. And since Geean was aware of its location, he didn't have to be the slightest bit stealthy about it.

He must assume for the moment that he couldn't escape from Naze, and that Geean would arrest him whenever it pleased him.

The sun was high in the heavens when he reached the fifth columnist part of the city. He recognised a street, then another, then he realised that he was near the apartment. As he hurried eagerly forward, a young woman's familiar voice whined:

'Your blood, mister.'

Slade was walking on, when a gasp escaped the girl. He whirled, and stared at her. Her face was already stiffening to the encounter.

'Well,' she said with a faint sneer, 'if it isn't the man who was going to destroy Naze.'

Slade said, 'Amor!' Then he remembered Geean, and that

his movements were probably being observed. 'Quick,' he said, 'meet me at Caldra's apartment. I'll give you some blood then. But now – slap my face as if you're mad at me.'

She *was* quick. Her hand came up and dealt him a stinging blow on the cheek. She swaggered away, and he walked on, for the first time beginning to realise the implications of what had happened. Amor – on the streets.

He had a sudden sense of personal degradation. Then anger against Leear. She was responsible for this.

He wondered bleakly if the girl would turn up at the apartment.

She was there ahead of him. She opened the door for him, and began to talk even as he crossed the threshold. She chattered with a mad speed. Her face was flushed, her eyes wide and staring. Her hands shook. She looked on the verge of a nervous breakdown.

She had escaped death the night Caldra was killed because she was not in the apartment. She had spent the night with a girl friend.

'I was afraid that I would go to your room if I stayed.'

The feverish way in which the words were spoken reminded Slade. He climbed to his feet, and went into her bedroom. The syringe and the cup lay on the table beside her bed.

He thought sickly, *To such depths can the potential Homo Superior sink.*

He took the syringe into the kitchen, boiled some water on one of the curious energy elements, and then sterilised the syringe needle. He inserted the needle into a vein in his left arm. The blood glittered darkly as it flowed into the transparent syringe. When it was full he squirted it into the cup. The liquid hissed a little as it touched the metal, but there was no reaction. With a steady hand, he set the cup down on the table beside her.

The girl licked her lips, but she did not look at the cup. Her face was stiff, her body rigid. Her eyes were looking fixedly at the floor. She said in a monotone:

'Why have you come back to the city?'

So she was beginning to think things over. It was a good sign. Slade began to talk. He was completely frank, though brief. When he had finished, Amor's eyes were gleaming. She stood up. She was suddenly enormously excited.

'This is it,' she said. '*This is it!*' She looked at him, wide-eyed. 'Don't you see, it's not an accident your being here. Everybody's being terribly clever but determined. Geean has let himself fall into the trap. Why? Because he feels safe behind his silver belt, but he's desperately anxious to find out how Leear thinks she can use you to destroy him. And in his bold fashion, he'll take risks now so that he'll know in the future.'

She had started pacing the floor, as she talked. Now, she stopped, directly in front of Slade. She said in an intense voice:

'Go straight to him. That will baffle him. He's expecting you to do something. He's expecting to tell you to do something. Very well, I'll tell you. Leear has said that only you can kill Geean. That means that nothing can happen until you are present.

'That means that you, under the present circumstances, have to seek him out. You can't escape it in the long run anyway. There is no escape from Naze except through Leear. And you may be sure that she'll keep you here now until you do what she wants. Besides, Geean will have you brought before him sooner or later anyway and – *Here!*'

She had raced off across the room. She came racing back carrying the cup of blood. She held it out to him. She said in feverish tone:

'Take a sip of this. It will give you courage. The effect of a sip won't last longer than an hour.'

Slade took the cup curiously. He felt overwhelmed. He had always intended to taste the stuff, though the idea of drinking his own blood was repellent. Nevertheless, he was not going to be rushed so swiftly into putting himself into the clutches of Geean. His impulse was to temporize.

He brought the cup to his lips, hesitated. And then he took a little swallow –

'Get in there,' the officer of the tower guard said insolently. 'If his excellency Geean decides to speak to you, he'll let you know.'

The door shut with a bang.

Slade staggered as he moved farther into the room. The sense of ecstatic, almost unbearable pleasure that had burst along his nervous system within seconds of his swallowing the blood, was gone now. What remained was a blurred memory of mad pleasure-dreams, and a gathering fury.

That little wretch, he thought, *that scoundrel, Amor. She knew what would happen.*

A sort of hypnotism it had been, driving him resistlessly through a mist of streets on wings of joyous excitement straight to the central tower of Geean. Blood drinkers must give their brains directional thoughts just before they drank.

His directions had been to go to Geean, and here he was.

Still dizzy, Slade looked around the room. There was a bed in one corner, and a large window slashed across the opposite wall. Slade peered shakily out of the window, and blinked. He was looking down into a depth of distance. He estimated seventy stories, and he was leaning forward to verify the height when the realisation struck into his brain that he was *able* to lean forward.

There was no glass in the window.

He retreated back into the room, shocked by his mental condition, that had made it possible, however briefly, for him to be unaware that the window was a hazard. Better lie down, he thought shakily.

He dreamed a miserable afterdrug type dream. In the dream, his body was flung out of an open window, to fall seventy stories to the ground below. He awakened, shivering, and then grew rigid:

A nith was standing beside his bed, its long powerful head projecting above him. Its three eyes staring down at him were pools of unnatural light. It saw that he was awake, but made no effort to move away. It said:

'Who told you to come here?'

It stood there waiting.

Vagueness. Slade's brain had been tensed for almost anything. But not language, not speech. The surprise was too great for ordinary adjustment. Caught completely off guard, his conscious mind temporarily suspended function.

It was not funny. His metabolism was affected. There was a rush of loose nervous energy through his body. Nausea came, followed by an inability to perform certain normal releasing reflexes like swallowing and blinking. The blood seemed to congeal behind his eyes, and his vision blurred sharply.

He had an acute conviction, not a thought but a fear, that he was going to be precipitated back to the other earth. The fear grew so monstrous that his first thought was able to come through. His dream – He would fall seventy stories if he was knocked out of this plane. The picturisation of that fall almost petrified his reason.

But the seconds passed, and nothing happened. His confidence returned. The nith's bear-cat head was only a foot away from his face, as it said:

'What is the plan to destroy Geean?'

There were several things about the speech that almost got Slade going again. It was not a speech. There was no sound at all. The creature was thinking at him. This was mental telepathy.

Slade lay stiff, striving to grasp the implications of a beast that had a better than human system of communication. Memory came of the wild animals that had watched him, and the wariness of the birds near the caves. Was it possible that they were all mind readers?

The thought ended. The nith was snarling threateningly. A great paw came up.

'What is the plan?'

In a synchronised jerk, Slade flung himself to the far side of the bed, and snatched his knife. Horribly afraid, he tumbled off the bed. Then he was on his feet, knife ready, backing towards the nearest wall.

'Careful,' he said, 'I'll sink this knife into you six inches at least.'

Afterwards, Slade was not clear as to what happened then. He was partly facing the window when a second nith walked in from the empty air of seventy stories above ground. It carried a foot-thick transparent weapon, which cast a pale reddish radiance towards the first nith. The beast must have died instantly, but it took more than a minute for the radiance to dissolve its great body into nothingness. The newcomer looked at Slade. It thought at him urgently:

'A traitor. We've been waiting patiently for Leear to give the word to kill him. But now, there's no time to waste. First, I'd better get rid of this — ' Slade didn't get the word it used to describe the weapon.

He watched as the animal dextrously split the instrument in two. Inside was a simple set-up built around a loose strip of metal about an inch by three inches by four. The nith's paw clutched the small object.

'Quick,' it said, 'put this in your pocket. Like this.'

It was not something about which Slade had any say. The animal bounded towards him. Before he could decide whether he was going to resist, it had slipped the metal strip into his left coat pocket. Slade watched as it jammed the two sections of what remained of the weapon under the bed.

It came erect with a jerk. 'They're coming for you,' it said tensely. 'Remember, there's no victory yet. What we have done so far we could have done years ago.

'*This is the crisis.*'

The door opened, and half a dozen soldiers came in. Without a word they led Slade out into a long, dim corridor and into an elevator. The nith followed. The elevator creaked upward about ten floors. Another corridor, then a door that opened into a spacious apartment.

A tall thin man with a powerful physique was standing looking out of a glassless window. He was dressed in the silver shining clothes of a hunter of Naze, and until he turned Slade had no sense of familiarity. It was that that made terrific the shock of recognition.

Geean was Malenkens.

CHAPTER ELEVEN

It was a morning of devastating shocks for Slade. He was aware of the great man watching him with a faint smile, and it was the contemptuous texture of that smile that finally pulled Slade out of his desperate turmoil.

In a burst of thought, he saw the picture. Danbar's apology. Explained now. Geean's nith that night at Caldra's apartment must have read his mind, and on the basis of the information it secured, Geean had been enabled to lay in wait for him at the cave village. There, without asking any questions, he had learned from Slade the detailed story of what had happened.

Bloodthirsty threats must have been used to silence so completely men like Danbar.

The other's smile was more satiric. 'You're quite right,' Geean said. 'That is what happened.'

The words, so accurately reflecting his thoughts, startled Slade. He looked at the nith, and its mind touched his instantly :

'Naturally, I am giving Geean a censored version of your thoughts. That is why he used the traitor nith. He had to have somebody who could read minds, and I was selected as a substitute because of my overall resemblance to the dead-one. But now, you must be on the alert.'

It went on with ill-concealed haste : 'Geean is not as calm as he appears. He has a tremendous respect for Leear, and something has already happened to make him realise that this *is* the crisis. If he should suddenly become afraid, he will kill you instantly.

'You must accordingly be prepared to act on a flash thought from me.'

'But what am I supposed to do?'

There was no answer to that intensely thought question. Slade licked dry lips, as the realisation penetrated how completely he was involved in the moment by moment developments. He thought, 'I've got to convince Geean, persuade him that I'm no danger.' Before he could speak, Geean said :

'Slade, you are alive at this moment because I am undecided. A woman' – his voice grew savage – 'named Leear, the only other silver belt immortal, has claimed that she can use you to kill me. I could murder you out of hand, but she would soon be able to produce another person like you with which to threaten me, and the next time perhaps I might not find out about it in advance. This is the time I must take any attendant risks. You are the man who benefits for the moment. Slade, I must find out what her method is. To me, nothing in the world matters as much.'

It was impressive. Geean's face had changed as he talked. Earnestness was in every line. The man was fascinated to the core of his soul by the threat to himself. He, who was immortal, was suddenly menaced, and the startling thing must be the vagueness, the lack of detail of that all-embracing menace. Hundreds of years had probably passed since Geean had experienced such an excitement of interest.

Slade's private thoughts ended, for Geean was continuing, his voice harder, his manner more intent:

'Slade, it is clear to me that you are an unwilling pawn in this affair. But I can do nothing about that. Here you are. The issue has been forced despite all my warnings to Leear. At this moment, and there is no question that it is her doing, an atomic fire is raging on the fortieth level of the tower. It will not be long before it reaches us up here.'

Briefly, Slade's attention wandered. He stood, startled. An atomic fire. Why, that meant the tower would be destroyed, the barrier would come down forever. Naze was already doomed.

In his mind's eye, he visualised that fire of fires. He began to tremble. The others undoubtedly had methods of escape, but what about him. The implacable voice of Geean went on:

'It has always been possible for Leear to start such an uncontrollable atomic reaction among the machinery of the barrier, but long ago' – his tone grew remote – '*long ago*, I warned her that if she ever did I would murder every human being on the planet.'

His eyes, as cold as glass, fixed Slade. The change in the man absolutely astounded Slade. At the beginning, he had had something in him of the stern kindly appearance of Malenkens. All gone now. His face was transformed. It was like a mask, so deadly, so cruel that Slade was taken aback. In the space of a few minutes Dr. Jekyll had become Mr. Hyde. Geean said in an infinitely savage voice:

'At all times Leear has known that if she destroyed the barrier I destroyed the race. She has made her choice. So it shall be.'

The words were so ultimately meaningful that they did not immediately make sense. Slade was thinking that the spectacle of Geean changing had been like being in the presence of a man who was drinking himself into a piglike state, like having a sudden glimpse of sewer, like being compelled to watch an obscene picture. Slade shivered with repulsion, and then, abruptly, his absorption with physical things passed. In one jump, the immense meaning of the man's words penetrated.

He felt half paralysed, and then, stronger than before the realisation came that he must convince Geean, must persuade him that Michael Slade would do nothing to injure him. He parted his lips to speak – and closed them again.

A shape was walking into the window behind Geean. It was a woman's shape, momentarily insubstantial. The nith must have warned Geean, for he turned mustering a grimace of a smile. The smile became a broad sneer as Leear came into the room.

Slade looked at her stiffly. He had an idea that his life was hanging in the balance. Now that Leear had arrived, Geean must be tensing to the necessity of dealing swift death to the one man who was supposed to be able to kill him. The nith's tremendously anxious thought impinged upon his mind:

'Relax, man, for your sake and ours. Surely, you have enough experience now with the nature of the nervous system to realise that an unrelaxed man is at a terrible disadvantage. I assure you that I will give you some warning. So be calm, and face this deadly situation.'

Relax! Slade clutched at the hope. Relaxation should be easy to him now. The hope went deeper, farther. What a tremendous and terrible joke on Geean was the presence of this nith.

Slade looked at the animal in a great wonder. There it sat on its haunches, a gigantic cat bear, reading everybody's thoughts, passing on to each person a censored version of what it saw. And Geean believed – stood there, cold and confident, and *believed* – that it was his nith.

If he was really unkillable, then that delusion meant nothing. But if Leear had a method of killing him, if there was a weakness in his impregnability, then Geean had made the mistake of his career.

Slade drew a long, deep breath, and let it out – long. Relaxation was as swift as that. Standing there, he had his first good look at Leear.

It was a different Leear than he remembered from his brief glimpses. She had been nude beside the marsh, and little more than a shadow inside the spaceship. Somehow, he had taken it for granted that she wore the rough and ready clothes of the cave dwellers.

He was mistaken. No cavewoman was here. Her hair was a braided marvel, not a loose fringe, not a straggling curl. And it glowed with a lacquer-like luster. She wore a silkish garment that seemed brand new. And it must have been designed for her. It showed off her figure with an almost demure good taste. Even her dominating attitude was softened, for she sent a quick warm smile at Slade, and then, as she faced Geean squarely, the smile faded. If she intended to speak, she was too slow. Geean it was who broke the silence:

'All decked out in your bridal finery,' he sneered. He began to laugh. It was a loud, insulting laughter. He stopped finally, and turned grinning to Slade. 'You will be interested to know, my friend, that you are the last hope of this ten thousand year old spinster. It is a little difficult to explain, but the cavemen, by very reason of their type of nerve training, are adversely affected by the aura of a woman who gains her nerve power by mechanical means. Accordingly, she cannot get a husband for herself among them. That leaves my blood drinkers out there' – he waved a hand towards the window – 'and you.'

The grin was wider. 'For reasons of morality, she is not interested in a man who has formed the blood drinking habit, which of course narrows the field down to you. Amusing, isn't it?'

The grin faded. Abruptly savage, the man whirled on Leear. 'And you, my dear,' he said scathingly, 'will be interested to know that Slade is on my side, not yours. The nith has just informed me that he is desperately anxious to convince me that I have nothing to fear from him. Since it will inform me when and if he changes his mind, I find myself in a unique bargaining situation.'

He didn't realise. It was amazing, it was almost staggering

to see him standing there accepting what the nith was telling him. Not that it told a lie about Slade's intentions and desires but the fact that it was quite coolly giving him real facts emphasised in a curious fashion how completely at its mercy he was for information.

For his own sake Geean had better be unkillable. Otherwise he was right behind the eight ball.

'We want to show you,' the nith's thought came. 'If Geean will let us, we want to show you what is behind this fight of the ship and the city. That is why I told him about your determination not to kill him.'

It went on swiftly, 'It will be a postponement only. You cannot escape the necessity of choosing between the two worlds at war here, the two people standing before you. I can tell you this much. When the moment comes your choice will be free, but only in the sense that anything in this universe is free.

'But now, we must persuade Geean to let you hear a brief history of Naze.'

Geean was quite willing. He looked genuinely amused. 'So it's really come down to persuading Slade to do something. I think I ought to warn you that at the moment I am the one who is the most likely to win him over. I've just been remembering some of the things he told me about his country. Only a few years ago they dropped atomic bombs on major cities of some enemies of theirs. The parallel to our own case is most interesting, and augurs so ill for you that I would suggest you simply open your mind to the nith, and so get the whole affair over with as swiftly as possible. All I want to know is, how did you plan to use him to kill me?'

He smiled. 'You won't do it? Very well, let's get it over with. It always amuses me to hear biased accounts of events in which I have participated.'

He walked over to a couch, and sat down. And waited.

Leear turned towards Slade. 'I shall be quick,' she said.

It was not a long story that she told then. But it was the picture of the end of a civilisation that had attained mechanical perfection. The immortal inhabitants of Naze were indestructible by virtue of their silver belts, which gave them nerve control. There were machines for every purpose, and all worked on the same principle – control of the human nervous system by means of inorganic energies.

As the slow years passed, the very perfection began to pall. It was discovered that individuals were beginning to commit suicide. Boredom settled like a vast doom over that ultimate materialistic civilisation, and with each passing day men and women sought surcease in voluntary death.

It became a mass tendency. In the beginning, the planet had been well-populated, almost overcrowded. At the end a handful of millions lived in eighteen cities. It was into this impasse that new discoveries about the human nervous system projected a whole new outlook on the future of man.

Experiments were performed on animals and birds. In an amazingly short time various breeds were able to read minds, something which man, with all his machines, had never been able to accomplish. They reacted marvelously in other ways also, and so a plebiscite was held, and it was decided by an overwhelming vote to put aside artificial immortality and give the new wonderful science a chance.

Leear paused and looked at Slade gravely. 'There could be no half measures. It was all or nothing, no volunteer system could be permitted, no exceptions. The new discoveries proved that man, in his primitive simplicity, had followed the wrong road to civilisation, and and that he must retrace his steps and make a new beginning. He must go back and back away from the materialistic gods he had followed so long away from his cities and his machines. You yourself have seen what men like Danbar can do, and he has attained only a part of the third or molecular phase of control. The final, electronic phase, impossible of attainment so long as the city of Naze exists, goes completely beyond anything that has ever been envisaged by man. With our mechanical belts, our silver belts, we have had tantalising glimpses, but that is all. Men will be as gods, almost omnipotent, and naturally immortal.

'Do you hear me? *Naturally immortal!* In your world and my own, long ago, thousands of generations of human beings have died unnecessarily. All of them had within their own bodies the power of powers, the innate capacity to realise their every desire.'

The picture had been growing on Slade, as she talked. The existence of the cavemen was explained. Odd pieces in the jigsaw puzzle of this world were beginning to fit into place, and he had a sudden dazzling vision of what she was getting at.

164

Leear was continuing, swiftly: 'Think of your own experience,' she said in an intense voice. 'You came from one plane of existence into another because your mind suddenly accepted a new reality. And then there is a comparison that shows how completely wrong appearances can be. Light. The people of the two-eyed world must have a definition of light as something materialistic, something external.'

She stared at him so demandingly that Slade nodded, and gave the wave and corpuscular theories of light.

'Light,' said Leear triumphantly, 'is a perception of the reactor, not an activity of the actor. Out there in space is a great body we know as the sun. We and every object in this room, whether organic or inorganic, are aware of the presence of that sun. We all react to its presence, just as it reacts to ours. But it sends us no heat, no light, *nothing*. The awareness is inside ourselves, inside the molecules of this table and that chair. To us, that awareness manifests as a perception which we call light. Now, do you see, now do you realise that primitive man, unaided, followed the wrong course. He had no way of understanding the true nature of his world.'

Slade hadn't expected to grasp her meaning. But he did. Only a few months before, he had attended a lecture by a disciple of Einstein. And in a distorted fashion, *this* was the famous scientist's latest theory of light. He had forgotten all about it.

He was frowning over the visualisation, when he happened to glance at Geean. That brought him back with a start to an entirely different kind of reality. He said:

'Where does Geean fit into all this?'

Geean said dryly, 'I was just going to ask that question myself.'

Leear was silent for a moment. Then, in a low voice:

'There was opposition, of course, to the great plan. All silver belts had been destroyed except those of myself and my companion who had been chosen by lot to man the ship which you saw, to watch over the experiment, to chronicle its progress, and –'

She stopped. 'There was opposition,' she said, flatly. 'A small, selfish minority led by Geean –'

Again, she stopped. This time Geean laughed, but the laughter ended abruptly. He said somberly:

'They had no idea how far I had decided to go.'

Something of the remorselessness of the decision he had

carried out then came into his face, and into his voice, as he went on:

'My forces struck one night at the seventeen cities, and wiped them out with atomic bombs. By a trick we secured the belt of Leear's companion, and killed him. That is the belt I now wear. We had planned also to destroy the ship, but by pure accident Leear had taken it from its berth.'

He breathed heavily with the memory of what must have been the shock of shocks of his long, ruthless life. His eyes were narrowed to slits, his body tense.

'She attacked our storehouse in Naze. By the time we got the barrier up, she had destroyed all chance of our ever making more belts.'

Geean gave a final reminiscent shudder, and then straightened slowly. He looked around belligerently. 'Enough of this,' he said. 'I can't quite imagine a stranger to this world getting so heated over something that happened more than a thousand years ago, that he will risk his life to avenge it.'

So quickly did the conversation sink to practical verities.

CHAPTER TWELVE

It was too long, Slade thought gaily. Too many centuries had passed since that collossal crime had been perpetrated. And yet, in spite of the vast time gap, something of the horror of it reached across the years and touched him.

For the problem was still here. *Here*, in this room. The struggle for ascendancy between the ship and the city. That collective entity the ship was going to defeat the entity that was the city. But Geean would survive; and, by that very survival, he would retain the power of death over all the defenseless people of this plane.

But life centred in the individual. A man must save himself.

'You are wrong,' thought the nith. 'Life is the race. The individual must sacrifice himself.'

That was too deep for Slade. He grew aware that Geean was still speaking, at him now:

'My mind reading animal,' he said, 'has been keeping me in touch with your thoughts. I'm happy to note that you dismiss Leear's arguments as so much impractical metaphysics. It's possible,' he went on, 'that you and I are closer together mentally than I have suspected. The nith has also told me of the arguments you are marshaling to convince me that I ought to keep you alive. Frankly, I hadn't really thought about your ability to go to your earth as being valuable to me, but I can see how it might be.'

Slade, who hadn't even thought of any arguments to save himself, stared at the nith in amazement. It was startling to realise that the beast had been using a skillful psychology to save his life.

'I told you,' the nith thought into his mind, 'that, when the moment came, your choice would be personally free. He has decided that, if no crisis occurs, he will let you live.'

Slade's answering thought was grim. 'But how am I going to get down to the ground?'

'That,' flashed the nith, 'comes under the heading of what I said before. No choice in this universe is absolutely free. You can trust yourself on our side, or you can make arrangements with Geean.'

So that was it. They thought they were going to force

him to take one risk to avoid another. And when you got right down to it, they pretty well had him. Slade thought savagely:

'What do you want me to do?'

'Geean must die. Only you can kill him.'

'I've heard that all before.' Impatiently. 'What I mean is –'

He stopped. For weeks he had known that this was what would be required of him. The realisation had lain there in the back of his mind, to be occasionally brought forward and pondered in an unreal fashion. It was altogether different to think suddenly, '*This* is the moment.'

He who had never killed a man must now kill Geean.

How?

You have in your left hand pocket an instrument. Turn slowly until your left side is pointing at Geean. Put your hand surreptitiously into your pocket and press the button that you will find right at the top of the device.

That instrument has now had time to integrate itself to your nervous system, a nervous system which, as you know, is not yet completely stabilised in this plane. When you press the button, it will transmit to Geean in a very concentrated form your present instability. He will be instantly projected to the two-eyed plane of existence, and will fall eighty stories to the ground. Just as your bullets would not work when you first came here, so his silver belt will be valueless there.

Slade could feel himself changing colour. He was vaguely aware that Leear and Geean were talking sharply to each other, but his mind couldn't begin to focus on them. Do that, he was thinking, to anybody.

He remembered his own fear of such a fall. And suddenly a horror came.

Just a minute. If I'm involved in this process of transferring from one plane to another, then I'll fall too.

No, you won't.

He didn't believe it. With a hot terror he saw the whole picture. This was what all that stuff about sacrificing the individual for the race had been leading up to. In his mind, he saw the bodies of Geean and himself hurtling down and down. And it built a curious kinship between himself and the man.

'I swear,' said the nith, 'that you will not die.'

Utter disbelief came.

168

And utter dismay.

The nith was desperate. 'You are forcing us to extremes. Leear has decided that either she or Geean dies here today. If you do not kill Geean, then, unless he wins a complete victory, he will carry out his threat to destroy every man and woman and child on the planet. You can see that Leear cannot permit that to happen. Accordingly, the choice is yours. What you do will determine finally whether the people of this planet shall become slaves of Geean or whether they will have the opportunity to realise their natural potentialities.'

Slade thought hesitantly, 'You mean Leear is going to kill herself.'

The nith was satirical. 'Please do not concern yourself about Leear. Concern about her is a moral characteristic, shall we say a racial as distinct from an individual, think-only-of-oneself characteristic. It is purely in your mind, having no external reality. What does it really matter if this woman and all that she stands for dies, provided you live?'

It must have despaired of convincing him in time. It must have projected a thought towards the woman. For she turned even as Geean, narrow-eyed with suspicion, was saying, 'Unless you leave here this minute, I shall have to revise my decision about not killing Slade.' She turned, and she said to Slade:

'Please, my friend, think of the generations that have been imprisoned in this city. Think of Amor, of —'

She stopped hopelessly. 'You force me,' she said, 'to the final sacrifice.'

Her hands moved to her waist, and disappeared under her blouse. They came out again instantly dragging a thin belt. She flung it viciously. It flashed with a silvery metallic fire as it fell to the rug.

'Your silver belt!'

It was Geean who shouted the words, piercingly. Never in his life had Slade heard such a yell of mixed triumph and unbelief. The man literally staggered forward and snatched up the belt. His eyes were glassy and, briefly, quite myopic with ultimate pleasure. He began to run towards the wall to Slade's left. There was a coneshaped gadget in the near corner. With trembling fingers Geean stuffed the belt into it.

169

It flared with a vivid fire, and was consumed in one puff.

Slowly, then, the man's sanity came back. He shook himself. He faced the room, and looked from Leear to Slade, and his face showed a mounting consciousness of the extent of his victory.

'Ah,' he said ecstatically, 'I am at last in a position to decide what I'm really going to –'

Slade never learned what Geean was in a position to decide. He was shocked to the core of his being. Actually, Leear's appeal on Amor's behalf had convinced him. The memory of Amor's degradation had brought a vivid picture of a people held down by a devil-like egotist.

He had turned automatically to follow the man's movements. His hand was in his pocket, and his left side towards Geean. He was thinking that under certain circumstances a man's free choice must include the possibility of personal death.

With a tiny pressure, he pressed the activating button of the gadget in his pocket.

STATEMENT TO THE CORONER'S JURY
By DETECTIVE LIEUTENANT JIM MURPHY

When the body of Michael Slade was discovered last week in the foothills near the city of Smailes, I was dispatched to the scene. It was at my request that the inquest hearing was transferred to Mr. Slade's home city, where most of the witnesses lived.

About these witnesses, I wish to say that all of them, without exception, were doubtful about identifying the deceased as Michael Slade when they were first shown the body. Later, on the stand, they were more positive, having apparently resolved their earlier doubts on the basis of 'The dead man is three-eyed. Therefore it must be Michael Slade.'

One of my reasons for going to Smailes was to make some attempt to find out where Michael Slade had been during the past few months.

I have considerable experience at locating missing persons, but my usual methods produced no results whatever. While the time elapsed since Mr. Slade's death has been very short, I am almost prepared to say that further search will only emphasise the following fact:

Michael Slade walked out of his own back yard in this

city several months ago, and his body was discovered last week near the city of Smailes. There is no record of his whereabouts during the interval.

They climbed towards the top of the spire ahead of the ominous hum and crackle of the fire. The direction worried Slade. How were they going to get down, with flames barring the lower levels? And suppose that the fire ate through the main walls, and the upper part of the immense building toppled to the ground far below.

There was a possibility, of course, that she and the nith could get down as easily as they had come in through the windows. But Leear shook her head when Slade asked if that was to be the way.

She stopped near a window. 'We came,' she said, 'by means of my silver belt. I've been hoping to run into a storeroom of fliers. If we don't find any, then you are our only hope.'

'Me?' Slade was startled.

She said, 'Tell me, can you visualise in your mind the wheel machine which you hid in the brush near where you were captured by the hunters of Naze?'

Slade gave her an astounded look. So she had known about that. At last, he said, 'I think so.'

She persisted, 'Including the three bright spots?'

This time he merely nodded, for he was beginning to remember what it could do.

'Then be quick,' said Leear. 'Its top speed is limited, something under two thousand miles an hour. It will take several minutes to get here.'

Slade stared at her, and swallowed hard. But he walked with her to the window, closed his eyes, and pictured the wheel machine. The memory was blurred for a moment, then it came sharp and clear.

Standing beside him, Leear said softly, 'Blink slowly, and don't strain to hold the picture of it. Let it wax and wane. All this is unimportant in a way, because, during the next six years, both you and I must learn the natural ways.'

That pulled him. That caught at his brain. That tore him from his concentration. He pictured himself as he might be six years hence – it was her gentle, almost hypnotic voice that pressed him back.

'Hold it,' she said quickly, '*hold* it! It will sink to Earth if you don't, and there is no time to waste. Any minute now the main barrier machinery will be reached, and then the barrier will go down. After that, even the tough materials of the spire will not stand long.'

Her words steadied Slade. Away in the back of his mind was a memory of what Geean had said about bridal finery. An edge of worry shadowed his mind. Because, when you came right down to it, a man did not marry a woman ten thousand years older than himself. Amor, yes. Her failings were human, normal, forgivable. He had a feeling the girl would be willing to become his companion. He would certainly ask her.

He was so intent on the wheel machine that he missed entirely a little byplay beside him. The nith informed Leear of what Slade was thinking. The woman hesitated, then her features began to change. Her face was taking on a startling resemblance to the face of Amor when a fierce thought from the nith arrested the process:

'Don't be a fool,' it said sharply. 'At the moment he will not take kindly to the idea that you were Amor. You assumed that role in order to give him a sympathetic picture of a girl of Naze. He would have been shocked by the character of a real blood-drinking girl. At the moment he might blame you for the death of Caldra, even though you had gone away expecting that Caldra would try to take blood from him, and so precipitate him back to his own plane.

'Another thing,' the nith went on, 'I have noticed in your mind that you are responsible for his having been born a three-eyed mutation in a two-eyed world. Do not tell him that immediately either. Let him discover later that you have controlled his life from an early embryo stage. Let him find out later that you can be all woman –'

The woman was hesitating. Abruptly, she became Leear again. She saw the wavering of the purple carrier. She let out a very femininelike squeal. 'The barrier,' she cried, 'it's down.'

Her words were like a cue. There was a flash of metallic brightness in the distance. The wheel machine came through the open window, and jerked to a stop in front of Slade's eyes.

'The nith first,' said Leear urgently. 'Then me, then you. And don't worry. It floats swiftly.'

It was almost swift enough. The last time he brought it towards his eyes the roar of the fire was a hideous sound in his ears. He climbed into the flowershaped wheel, shoved hard – and hung on.

The sun was a bright glory almost directly overhead. There were many people below, but as Slade drew near to the ground, he could still see no sign of either Leear or the nith. A tall, slim young woman put her arms towards him, and with a start Slade recognised Amor. He shouted at her, and she waved back, frantically.

He came presently into a city that was already quaveringly conscious of its destiny.

THE VERDICT OF THE CORONER'S JURY

It is the unanimous decision of the jury that there can be no doubt that the dead body is that of Michael Slade. The unusual clothes cannot be regarded as important, and the jury therefore finds that Michael Slade met his death as a result of a fall from a height, very possibly from an airplane. There is no evidence of foul play or murder.

Also Available in Sphere Books:

STAR WARS

George Lucas

A spectacular motion picture from
Twentieth Century-Fox!
Luke Skywalker challenged the storm
troopers of a distant galaxy on a daring
mission – where a force of life became the
power of death!!
Farm chores sure could be dull, and Luke
Skywalker was bored beyond belief. He
yearned for adventures out among the stars
– adventures that would take him beyond
the furthest galaxies to distant and alien
worlds.
But Luke got more than he bargained for
when he intercepted a cryptic message from
a beautiful princess held captive by a dark
and powerful warlord. Luke didn't know
who she was, but he knew he had to save
her – and soon, because time was running
out.
Armed only with courage and with the light
sabre that had been his father's, Luke was
catapulted into the middle of the most
savage space-war ever . . . and he was
headed straight for a desperate encounter
on the enemy battle station known as the
Death Star!

0 7221 56693

THE HUMANOIDS

Jack Williamson

"We serve and obey, and guard men from harm."

Those were the words that scientist Clay Forester had learned to dread. Those words were the code of the Humanoids – and the Humanoids had enslaved his world! Sleek, invincible, perfect machines, the Humanoids had been created to fulfil an ideal, but the ideal had got out of hand. Now they followed their Prime Directive with terrifying insistence. Men must be safe, so dangerous activities such as driving, flying – even walking unescorted – were forbidden. Men must be happy – so any dissatisfaction was removed with the aid of a hypodermic needle. Man was a helpless prisoner. Clay Forester could not rest until he had destroyed the robot invaders. But it seemed he was powerless to fight them – until a child with an incredible talent walked into his plans . . .

THE HUMANOIDS is a classic SF novel in the masterful tradition of Isaac Asimov's ROBOT series.

SCIENCE FICTION   0 7221 9176 6

All Sphere Books are available at your bookshop or newsagent, or can be ordered from the following address:
Sphere Books, Cash Sales Department,
P.O. Box 11, Falmouth, Cornwall.

Please send cheque or postal order (no currency), and allow 19p for postage and packing for the first book plus 9p per copy for each additional book ordered up to a maximum charge of 73p in U.K.

Customers in Eire and B.F.P.O. please allow 19p for postage and packing for the first book plus 9p per copy for the next 6 books, thereafter 3p per book.

Overseas customers please allow 20p for postage and packing for the first book and 10p per copy for each additional book.